"I'm Glad You're Here With Me Tonight, Isabelle. *Whatever* The Reason."

"Tony, try to keep an employer-employee view. That's all it can be between us. Unless, of course, you decide to become a marrying man." She suspected that a woman looking for a husband was the last person Tony would want to spend time with.

"I'm *not* a marrying man. But we can still enjoy an evening out," he replied smoothly.

Isabelle wished she could remain as cool as he was. "I want a family, so our association outside of work isn't a good idea."

"We'll see about that one," he said, smiling at her. "I *know* you know how to enjoy life. I have a very good memory."

Dear Reader,

A Lone Star Love Affair touches on one of my favorite topics—families. I've always been deeply involved with my family. Therefore, family themes run through many of my stories, with parents, children, siblings and other relatives included in the plots.

This time the goals that many have of wanting a family or hoping for success in business are the driving forces of the hero and heroine. In both situations, the goals are family-oriented, coming out of each person's background.

Beautiful, blonde Isabelle Smith is captivated by Tony Ryder, a dynamic, handsome multimillionaire who is driven to become a billionaire by forty. There's no room in Tony's life for marriage or children until he achieves that goal. Tony in turn is dazzled by Isabelle and wants her in his life, but on his terms.

With an overbearing father and a sister he protects and cares about, Tony thinks his goal is absolutely necessary for happiness. Because of her family, Isabelle's motivations clash totally with Tony's, and both fight the attraction they feel every time they are together.

Now you will get to know another one of the handsome millionaires who have been friends since earliest childhood—Nick, Jake, Tony and Gabe. *A Lone Star Love Affair* is a Texas story with the pitfalls, upheavals and problems two people work through because of love.

Thank you for letting me share this story with you.

Sara Orwig

SARA ORWIG

A LONE STAR LOVE AFFAIR

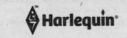

Recycling programs
for this product may
not exist in your area.

ISBN-13: 978-0-373-73111-4

A LONE STAR LOVE AFFAIR

Copyright © 2011 by Sara Orwig

www.Harlequin.com

Printed in U.S.A.

Books by Sara Orwig

SARA ORWIG

lives in Oklahoma. She has a patient husband who will take her on research trips anywhere from big cities to old forts. She is an avid collector of Western history books. With a master's degree in English, Sara has written historical romance, mainstream fiction and contemporary romance. Books are beloved treasures that take Sara to magical worlds, and she loves both reading and writing them.

With thanks to Stacy Boyd, Melissa Senate,
Shana Smith and Maureen Walters.

One

Tony Ryder couldn't suppress his jubilation.

It had taken years for him to acquire Morris Enterprises. Years—plus being in the right place at the right time.

Late at night, he had stepped off the elevator on the nineteenth floor of the twenty-story glass Morris building in downtown Dallas. Wall lights shed a softened glow in the empty corridor as he passed open doors. His father had made offers over the years for this company and never succeeded in acquiring it. Now one giant coup would make his controlling father back off. That made all the hours of work more than worth his efforts. Tony was growing as wealthy as his father and finally gaining the man's respect.

Tony had grown more pleased with the offices from the lobby to the top floor. Strolling the empty hallway, he paused to look at framed awards mounted on the beige walls. Farther along was a glass-enclosed case of trophies for graphic arts achievements. He noticed the same director's name on several awards and trophies. Moving on, he passed through open doors into a darkened office and switched on the light. He was in the graphic arts sector—a part of the company that he would change drastically. He intended to retain a few of the graphic arts people and offer the others generous severance packages, absorbing the remaining employees into his own public relations department.

He shut the light and continued along the silent, dimly lit hall, turning at the next open door into an anteroom. Light spilled inside from a doorway. Crossing the anteroom, Tony entered another spacious, elegant office. He stopped abruptly as a blonde looked up.

"Sorry, I didn't mean to startle you," he said, surprised and curious to find someone working after ten. His first thought was that he was looking at his most gorgeous employee. As she stood, his gaze drifted swiftly over her. In an all-business navy suit and matching silk blouse, she looked as if she had just arrived at work instead of putting in extra hours. Her blond hair was secured in a roll on the back of her head. He had the strange feeling of meeting her before, but he knew he would have remembered her. A sizzling current startled him. He was caught in wide blue eyes that darkened and mesmerized. Silence stretched until he realized they were entrapped in each other's gaze. When she touched a paper on her desk, the spell broke.

"You're working late," he remarked.

"I believe you, too, are working late," she replied.

He stepped forward to extend his hand across her desk. "Sorry, I'm Tony Ryder."

"Isabelle Smith," she said. "I know who you are." Her hand was slender, warm, and should have been like other feminine handshakes. Instead, the electric current he had first experienced just at the sight of her, magnified. Startled by his intense reaction, he focused intently on her, momentarily immobilized by his reactions.

"I'm here because I had something to finish. You're visiting rather late," she said. "Looking over your new acquisition?"

While her voice was neutral, her eyes were cool and assessing. He sensed she did not approve of him.

"You're right. And you're the Morris graphic arts department director."

"You've either done some homework about the business you just bought, or read the sign on my door." She walked around the desk and motioned to a chair. "Please have a seat," she said, taking a leather chair that was turned to face him. As she moved closer, he caught a whiff of exotic perfume. "I don't know whether you actually get involved or have staff who do that for you."

"I have staff, but I also want to be knowledgeable about my investments," he said as he sat near her. She crossed her legs and he couldn't resist one swift glance that made him want to look back for a thorough assessment. She had long, shapely legs. "I'm involved in whatever I own. What's so urgent to keep you working this late when you know your department will be split up?"

"So the rumors are true," she remarked, the frostiness in her tone increasing. "I intend to finish a few projects because we've already signed contracts. That won't change with the new management. I feel I need to wind things up before you actually take charge."

"You say that as if doomsday approaches."

She shrugged a slender shoulder. "That seems to be your approach to your acquisitions. I've done my homework and you have a reputation."

"Do I now?" he asked, amused. "Tell me what this reputation is."

"Ambitious. Driven. What I might label 'smash and grab.'"

He tried to bite back a smile. "I never thought of my actions in such a manner."

"I'm sure I'm not winning kudos with my new employer, but

I suspect it really doesn't matter what I say. I imagine you've already made decisions about the direction you will go."

"How would you describe yourself? You work far into the night. You're a director. Ambitious? Driven?"

She smiled faintly. "Touché."

"So we are both workaholics—there are rewards. Regarding the future of the company, I change only what I feel needs changing. As a director, you'll retain a position if that relieves your mind."

"'A position'—but not necessarily a director? I know changes are coming. I have a feeling you've looked into my background."

"So is your family patiently waiting at home?" he asked, having already noticed the absence of a wedding band. Her manicured nails were long. Everything about her looked precise, immaculate, professional. Keeping a barrier around herself, she was reserved with him. She made no effort to hide her resentment of his purchase of the company.

"I'm single. You make the news enough for me to know that you are, too."

"The single life lends itself to becoming a workaholic. There are far less distractions."

"You view a family as a distraction." Even though she spoke in the same tone, her disapproval had obviously escalated.

"At this point in life, family is not for me, because I'm wound up in business. Evidently, not for you, either."

She gave him a frosty smile.

They were lightly sparring, yet he experienced a scalding attraction that she seemed to also feel—an odd combination he had never encountered. Challenges were always interesting and she was definitely one.

"Do you often work this late?" he asked, enjoying talking to her. She was a beautiful woman, yet she wore the suit as if it were armor, hiding her figure. He rarely received such a cool reception from a gorgeous, single woman, much less one who was his employee. He couldn't resist the urge to try to break through the puzzling wall she maintained. Was it all men? Or just him, because he had bought out her employer?

"Occasionally," she replied, tilting her head. "Do you usually work this late?"

"If necessary. I haven't seen the building and this is a good time to wander freely. It surprised me to find you working."

"You bought this company sight unseen?"

"The building, offices and layout weren't significant factors. It's the people, the departments and what Morris Enterprises is involved in. I'm sure you know that."

"Yet you'll change the people and the departments." Her voice held a touch of frost. Otherwise she sat still, poised, looking as if she discussed an ad campaign.

"Some things will change. I've just acquired three highly successful hotel chains, plus a restaurant chain and a trucking business. This will grow my business. Even as we absorb this company, I think we can enlarge Morris Enterprises. You've built this department significantly—Morris has grown since you came on board. You have an impressive record," he said, recalling being briefed on Morris executives' performance reports. He'd decided then that she held potential, but he would move her down the corporate ladder because she would be going into a larger company. In spite of the compliment, he could not get a smile from her.

"Thank you. No one seems to know when you'll actually take over and begin changes."

"Soon. When I do, I'll interview the executives first," he said, unable to resist another swift glance at her legs.

"This encounter can almost count as my interview. You've asked some direct questions and I'm certain you've formed an opinion."

She was direct, straight-forward and not the least intimidated to be talking to the new owner of her company. She continued, coolly composed, yet along with their matter-of-fact conversation, he felt an undercurrent of awareness.

Amused again, he shook his head. "No, you'll have your formal interview. This is just a late-night chat, nothing more."

"Why do I think you've already made your decisions?" Big blue eyes stabbed into him.

"I can have an open mind. On the other hand—can you? Morris sold the company to me. I didn't do any arm-twisting." He couldn't resist another brief glance at her long legs. What would she be like when she let down all the barriers?

"You came to him with an offer he couldn't refuse and you knew he has been on the verge of retirement for the past three years." This time she didn't hide the frost. Her voice conveyed a cold anger.

"Can you blame me? This is a first-rate company."

She looked away and he studied her profile, long thick eyelashes, flawless peaches-and-cream skin, a straight nose—looks that would be unforgettable. Again it crossed his mind that they had met before, yet how could he forget her? If he had met her, the recollection would come.

"If you'll excuse me, it's late. I think I'll close for tonight," she said, standing.

Amused that he was being dismissed by her, as he stood, he asked, "Can I give you a ride home?"

She shook her head. "Thanks, no. I have my car."

"I'll see you out. I've been all through the building." He was unaccustomed to being brushed off by a woman where there was an obvious chemistry between them.

She smiled. "You don't have to see me to my car. This wasn't a date."

"I know I don't, Ms. Smith."

"It's Isabelle."

"And I'm Tony to my employees," he said. "I'll walk out with you. Then I'll know where to park when I come in Monday."

"I think you can find the parking spot that will have Reserved on a placard in front of the best space in the lot," she said.

He watched while she shut down her laptop and placed it in a bag that she shouldered. She pulled keys from the bag, switched off a desk light and turned toward the door. When he blocked her path, she looked up, wide-eyed.

"I wish now we'd met under other circumstances. You're definitely annoyed with me," he said.

"It won't matter. You have many interests and a sprawling enterprise that has absorbed this one. We'll rarely see each other. I hated to see Morris sold. You can't blame me for that."

"I think it's more than the sale," he said quietly, standing close enough to smell the perfume she wore. Her blue eyes were incredible, crystal clear, deep blue, thickly lashed. Glacial at the moment. When his gaze lowered to her mouth, he inhaled as he viewed full, heart-shaped lips, a rosy mouth that looked soft.

As he looked, her lips parted and he glanced into her eyes again. For an instant her guard had fallen and the look he caught was warm, receptive. It was gone in a flash as she gave a tiny shake while she passed him.

"It's very late, Tony…"

Against all human resources training, he reached out and touched her arm. "I don't have a policy against employees seeing each other off the job, dating, getting engaged or marrying."

Again that surge of electricity sizzled to his toes as she looked up sharply with a flash of fire in her eyes. But just as suddenly, the fire died and whatever she had been about to say was gone.

"Where I'm concerned, it won't matter."

"No deference to your employer?" he asked quietly, fighting an urge to ask her for a drink.

"Tony, it's getting late," she whispered, and broke away. He had seen the pink rise in her cheeks. Why was she fighting him and so angry with him? He hadn't moved her out of her job yet.

Puzzled over the degree of her animosity, he walked with her to the elevators. He pushed a button before she could reach it and they rode down in silence.

He could feel the barriers back in place, the chill in the air between them.

"I saw your ad campaign for the Royal Garden chain. It was well thought out and successful. Bookings jumped after the television ads started," he said.

"Thank you from my staff and me. They did an excellent job."

"Do you ever take full credit for anything?" he asked, looking at silky strands of blond hair wound in a roll and wondering how she would look with her hair unpinned.

"If I'm the only one to work on it. Otherwise, I don't deserve to take all of the credit."

"Will there ever be a time you can see me in any way other than your employer?"

"Of course. If I leave Morris, or if you do," she answered sweetly, and he smiled.

When the elevator doors opened, he stepped back to let her exit. He fell into step beside her and they both greeted the night security guard before going outside. Tony crossed the parking lot with her to her car.

"I hope you give my company a chance," he said. "I have the feeling you've already formed an opinion and have one foot out the door."

"Not yet," she said, as she clicked her key to unlock her car. While he held her door, she slid behind the wheel.

"I'll see you next at the reception we're having for the executives Thursday evening. You will attend, won't you?"

"Certainly. I believe it's mandatory unless one is in the hospital."

"We all need to meet one another."

She gave him a doubting look as if she didn't believe a word he said.

"Good night, Isabelle," he said, wishing he could prolong the time with her.

"Good night," she replied.

When she started the engine, he walked to his car. As she drove past, her profile was to him and she never glanced around.

"Isabelle Smith," he said, mulling over her name and the past hour. The only things he knew for certain were that she didn't like him and she resented his buying out Morris.

He remembered another Smith he had known. She had been a freshman or sophomore in college and he had met her at a party when he had been on campus for a seminar. Her name hadn't been Isabelle and she had been a carefree, fun-loving, sexy woman. It had been an instant hot attraction that ended in a passionate night together even though she had been a virgin. A blue-eyed blonde with a resemblance to Isabelle Smith, but only a slight similarity and one he dismissed as swiftly as it came to mind. Partying with him, Jessie Smith had been wild, friendly and filled with fun. She had constantly smiled until passion replaced her smiles. He hadn't forgotten her and he didn't think he ever would. He couldn't recall her major or where she was from. Even though he had wanted to, he had never tried to contact her because she would have been too big a distraction in his life at the time. His focus had been on building his fortune. She had faded from his life, but never from his memory. That had been an unforgettable night. There was enough of a resemblance in coloring and name to give him the feeling he had met Isabelle Smith before tonight, but she definitely was no Jessie Smith.

His cell phone beeped, indicating a text from his sister.

As he climbed into his sports car, he paused to read her message. In minutes he headed home. When he entered his neighborhood, he slowed, driving beneath tall trees with thick trunks in one of the oldest areas in Dallas. Bare limbs interlocked overhead, bordering sweeping lawns of two- and three-story mansions. A high, wrought-iron fence surrounded Tony's property and with a code he opened iron gates. As he wound along the wide driveway, he saw a familiar sports car parked at the front.

He pulled into his garage and entered his house, going straight through to open the front door. A woman with a mass of curly black hair and thickly lashed dark brown eyes matching his stepped out of the parked car and dashed toward his door. She crossed the illuminated wide porch.

He closed the door behind his younger sister. "Sydney, what brings you on the run at this hour?" he asked, smiling at her. He loved his sister.

"Dad. He wanted to see me tonight. I need to talk to you, Tony."

"Sure. Let's go to the family room. Want something to drink?"

"Cranberry juice if you have it."

Several small lights came on automatically as they entered a large room that held comfortable leather furniture, a bar and a large fireplace. Tony crossed to the bar to get a cold beer for himself and juice for his sister.

As soon as he had a fire blazing, he picked up his beer and sat on a chair facing his sister, who sipped her juice. "Okay, let's hear it. What's Dad done now?" Tony asked.

"Tony, he's pressuring me to dump Dylan," she said, focusing worried brown eyes on her brother.

"So? Sydney, it's your life. Do what you want," Tony answered.

"It's not that easy." She looked away as if lost in thought. Her gaze returned to Tony. "Dad's threatened me. If I marry Dylan, he'll disinherit me."

"Dammit. That's drastic. He must have talked to my friend Jake's dad who held such a threat over Jake's head. Our dads are old friends and both control freaks. That's where Dad got this idea of threatening you. It worked with Jake because he married."

"That's not all. Dad will stop all support and I'm on my own to finish medical school. I may have to make a choice between med school and Dylan. If I have to choose, Dylan wins. Worst of all, Dad will cut me out of the family completely. 'Don't come home' and all that."

"Mom won't go along with any such ultimatum," Tony said, losing his temper with his interfering father.

"She already has. For once, Mom sat in with us when he talked to me."

"That's serious," Tony remarked, giving his sister his full attention. "I don't think I've ever had Mom step in to back up Dad. I'm shocked."

"Mom doesn't like Dylan. She thinks he's a nobody and will embarrass the family. Even worse, he's an artist who had to put himself through college by relying on scholarships. It doesn't matter to them that his grades are excellent or what it took to accomplish sending himself."

"Graphic art is a respectable career," Tony answered, thinking about Isabelle, although it had been years since he'd had any worries about his family having to accept a woman in his life. "This is partially why I work like crazy. He's beginning to back off with me—especially since I acquired Morris Enterprises— because I'm going to make more money than he has and he can see it. Syd, I'm finally getting respect out of him."

"I doubt if I can ever say that. I thought if I made it through medical school, I would, but I don't think that any longer. If you're sympathetic to me at all, it will only increase the tension between you and Mom and Dad. As for Dylan, he just isn't from our circle of friends and his family is low income with blue-collar jobs. I'm afraid Dad will try every way he can to give Dylan difficulty. He'll try to sabotage Dylan getting work, or staying with a company. He will try to keep him out of any family gatherings."

"I don't think so, Syd. He wouldn't do that to you."

"Tony, really," she snapped, glaring at her brother.

"You'll know in time. As for the other, I'm one-quarter of this family and I'm not cutting you out, so you can see me on holidays."

"If you're even in the country. Thank you for offering, though."

"And don't worry about med school. I can support you right now. I have the money and can easily and gladly do it. Just tell me how much and I'll write the first check tonight," Tony said, feeling as protective of his sister as ever. Seven years older than Sydney, he had spent his life looking out for her and being a buffer between his parents and her. They had always been close.

"I don't want you to do that. I didn't call you to get you to finance me."

"I can afford it. I want to. End of argument."

"Oh, Tony," she said, her eyes filling with tears as she jumped to her feet to run and hug him. "You are the best brother in the whole world."

"I can support you without missing the money." He set down his beer. "I'll get a check."

"You don't need to now. Dad hasn't done anything yet."

"Don't wait until he does something. Let me give you a check and you put this money away. Open a new bank account Dad knows nothing about with a bank where no one knows him. This is a big enough city that you can get away from Dad's scrutiny. The minute he cuts you off, you let me know and I'll take up supporting you. In the meantime, you'll have this to fall back on if you need it. I'll be right back."

She wiped her eyes. "You really are the best brother ever."

He left to get a check, filling it out and returning to take it to her. She was back in the chair, her long legs tucked beneath her. When Tony handed her the check, she looked up with wide eyes. "Tony, this is enormous. I don't need money like this yet."

"Take it and do what I told you. This way you can open that new account and you'll have money any time you need it."

"I can't take this much."

"Syd," he said sternly, giving her a look, and suddenly she smiled, folding the check.

"Thank you, best brother in the whole world."

"You're welcome," he remarked dryly. "I'd talk to Dad, but we both know it will do no good. He's stubborn and he's a control freak. The only thing that Dylan can ever do to wring respect from Dad is what I'm doing—make as much money as Dad. I had a running start with influential connections, a top-notch education and family money. Dylan has none of that."

"I know. He can never make the money Dad did, but I don't care."

"Have you told Dylan?"

"Not yet, but I will. I'll miss my family, but at least you're not cutting me out. It's getting bad between Mom, Dad and me."

"Sorry, Syd. Dad has really focused on you. For now, it's you and not me."

"He won't bother you. I think you've thrown him for a loop with this latest acquisition. He wanted that chain for years." She was quiet for a moment.

Then Tony said, "Since he found out about Morris, he hasn't interfered in my life. I don't think he ever expected me to make as much money as he does."

"I wish I could and get him to stop meddling," she said. "But my calling is in the medical field, not business. I can't make the money I'd need to gain his respect and stop his interference."

Tony squeezed her shoulder. "Do you really love Dylan?"

She turned wide brown eyes on her brother. "Yes. You've asked me before. Each time I tell you yes, I'm more certain and my love has grown stronger. I don't care about the inheritance.

We'll get along. I have faith in Dylan. His grades were tops. He has an excellent job with a big company and hopes someday to go into business for himself. Dad says Dylan is a nobody. Mom and Dad both want me to marry one of those boys I've grown up with, Paul, Jason, Will. I'm not in love with any of them. I don't want to marry them and they bore me." She waved her fingers at Tony. "Mom and Dad would like you to marry Emma or Darcy."

"The day the sun rises in the west," he remarked. "The folks haven't said anything about that to me for several years. This past year Dad's gotten quiet on all fronts."

"You're surpassing him in business and he never, ever expected that to happen. You can thank me, too, for taking their attention."

"I definitely thank you."

"I know Mom and Dad mean what they say. They both want us to have 'society marriages.' But I love Dylan and I'm going to marry him."

"Let Dylan know what Dad has threatened. Fill him in so he knows exactly what it means. If Dylan still wants to marry you, then he's been warned. Dylan seems to truly love you from all you've told me. I trust your judgment with him. The more he knows the more he'll be prepared to deal with whatever our father does."

"Tony, why do we have parents like this?"

"Look at my friends and their interfering dads—Jake and Gabe Benton, Nick Rafford. Dad's no worse than theirs. When we were growing up, their interference was effective. Now, it's not."

"Thank heavens! I don't want him running my life," she said. "I'm meeting Dylan in thirty minutes, so I need to go, but I just had to talk to you."

"Call whenever you want. You know I'm always here for you."

"Thank goodness," she said. "You always stand by me in a crisis and you've been there when I'm hurt."

Tony smiled at her. When he could, he protected her from their parents' interference, but it was impossible to always deflect their attention.

She finished her juice and jumped to her feet. "I better run. Thanks for listening. I feel so much better with your encouragement and support."

"Sure. I'll need yours sometime."

She gave him a smile. "That will be the day. Whatever they throw at you, you manage to overcome. Tony, thank you so, so much."

"Forget it. You're there for me. You come talk whenever you want," he said, draping his arm around her shoulders and giving her a light hug.

She smiled up at him, then her expression changed. "Tony, they'll try to get you to sever ties with me."

"Doesn't matter. You know I'll never do that."

"Thank you," she said quietly.

"Syd, I would think Dylan knows the graphic artists in the city. He probably knows the top one with Morris. Her name is Isabelle Smith."

"I've met her at parties Dylan and I have attended. I don't really know her except to say hi. We've talked a little. From what Dylan has said, she's very good and he admires her work. They're friends because of their mutual interest in art. Now she works for you. She's gorgeous," Sydney said, her eyes dancing. "Thinking of dating an employee?"

"I'm allowed. I'm just curious because they are both in the same field."

Sydney laughed. "I'll ask Dylan about her. Maybe sometime the four of us can go to dinner."

"Syd—" he said in a threatening voice, and they both laughed.

"Watch out. You'll get Dad on your case if you start seeing an artist. Actually, you won't. I think you've stopped him cold as long as you don't lose the fortune you've made."

"It's a damn big relief. You stop worrying so much. You and Dylan can weather Dad's interference. If you're really in love, it won't matter what Dad does."

"I hope not. He has a lot of influence."

At her car Jake held the door. "Don't pay too much attention to our parents. When Christmas comes, it may be a whole different story."

"If it's not, I can live with it. I can't live with losing you."

He smiled. "You'll get along. And I'm always here for you. Take care, Syd."

"Sure. Thanks for the check, but mostly thank you for being the brother you are."

As he entered the mansion, his thoughts returned to earlier and Isabelle Smith. He wanted to see her again. He definitely would have an interview with her. Since he'd acquired Morris, three executives had resigned. He guessed from her frosty manner that she was going to resign, too. It was a plus-minus prospect. He wanted her to stay. On the other hand, if she didn't, it might be less complicated to see her socially.

Now he was looking forward to Thursday evening's reception more than before.

Two

Isabelle gripped the steering wheel tightly. Her insides knotted. Tony Ryder was a page out of her past. He obviously had not remembered her, and nothing about her had jogged his memory. A night she wished she could forget. The most passionate night of her life, and one that she had never been able to understand.

A singular time in which she had acted in a totally uncustomary fashion. Had it been Tony who had triggered her responses? The spring night? The looming end of the semester? She could never account for her actions to herself.

One thing remained the same—the white-hot, sizzling attraction experienced by both of them. Even though she had tried to keep from responding in even the slightest manner to his magnetism tonight, she'd failed. He had felt the same witchery, revealing his responses in small ways.

His riveting looks and commanding presence made him larger-than-life to her. It was impossible to see him in any ordinary manner. When they were together, she could feel the rising heat they generated. The man probably went through life getting everything he wanted. Between his money, his looks, his background, his sharp mind—how could he fail in any undertaking?

She wanted him out of her life and she definitely wanted away from him. She hoped she'd have a new job and be gone from Morris without Tony having a clue who she was. No way did she want to work for Tony Ryder. Tony was clearly not into commitment and she was. She had read about him on business pages. He was a workaholic and obviously avoided long-term relationships. As she approached each birthday now, her yearning for a family and a love she could trust increased. She wanted a lifelong relationship while Tony did not have even long-term relationships.

She had told Tony she would attend the company party, but now she had second thoughts.

Finally at home, Isabelle turned on Beethoven, showered and changed into pajamas, and poured a tall glass of cold milk. She couldn't shake thoughts of Tony and their encounter tonight. Tony Ryder was even more handsome and appealing than he had been the night she had met him when she had been in college.

How could he forget someone he had slept with? It had been such a passionate night. She grew warmer just thinking about it before making an effort to put those memories firmly out of mind.

Of all people to buy out Morris Enterprises.

Mr. Morris had planned to work four more years and then sell the company when Tony had come along with a dream offer. How she wished Tony had found other interests. Four more years with Morris would have been great. Now her future was uncertain. She had to start fresh with a new company. She would lose clients and accounts she knew well.

When she had started at Morris, she had thought the company would never change hands. The original shipping business had started with the trucking company in the 1920s. In 1946, Morris opened the first hotel. Within two years it had become a Texas chain, and in a few more years, a national chain. As the company had continued to grow, the word with employees was that the Morrises would never sell. Until the current Morris, whose only son was immersed in the Beltway political scene. After Morris's daughter married a jet-setting Frenchman, she no longer had interest in the family business.

Change happened, especially nowadays when companies changed hands with the right offer. Probably due to her awards, the recognition she had received for achievements in her field, plus the large number of companies she had dealt with because of her job with Morris, she had three excellent job offers to consider.

Thursday night she would put in an appearance, speak to Mr. Morris, as well as those she was close to at Morris, and then leave. She didn't care to schmooze with Tony.

She sat down at the kitchen table with her milk and the file of papers from businesses that had made her offers. She had them in order of preference with first choice Tralear Hotels, Incorporated, the hotel chain where Vernon Irwin, the former president of Morris, was going. Vernon wanted her, as well as five other Morris employees, to move with him and he had made her a highly tempting offer.

She had to get away from Morris before Tony realized who she was.

When she went to bed, she had dreams about Tony Ryder. One of her first thoughts on waking in the faintly gray dawn—*would* Tony remember who she was? Even more unsettling—how would she say no to him when she remembered what it was like to be with him?

On Thursday, Tony entered the luxurious reception room on the top floor of the Morris building. A piano player provided background music and a buffet of hors d'oeuvres were on tables scattered along three walls. A crowd had already gathered. As his eyes swept the room, disappointment ruled, because he did not see Isabelle.

He spotted the table with Seymour Morris and Vernon Irwin, who had already taken another job as president of Tralear Hotels, Incorporated, a fast-growing hotel chain. Three vice presidents who were still on the Morris payroll were also at the table. Casually looking for Isabelle, Tony crossed the room to greet the former CEO and each executive.

"Join us, Tony. You can humor an old man and sit for a spell."

"I'd be glad to," Tony said, smiling at the white-headed CEO. "I've looked forward to getting to meet more Morris people."

"Excellent. We'll introduce you and your executive staff in an informal manner shortly. I'll officially turn everything over to you and go. Vernon will introduce the Morris executives."

"No need for you to rush away. I look forward to meeting them to put faces with names." Tony wanted to ask about one director in particular, but he refrained. Instead, as he conversed with those around him, he idly watched the crowd.

"Why don't we do the introductions and let me officially move on. I can turn it over to you and get these old bones home to bed."

"Yes, sir," Tony replied, biting back a smile at the references to old and tired because he had already discovered that Seymour Morris worked out daily and had for years. Seymour was into polo, swimming, racquetball and golf.

As he moved to the microphone with Seymour, a blonde caught his attention.

In a plain black knee-length dress, Isabelle stood out. How had he missed her? Or had she just arrived? His insides clenched and flames heated him. Looking gorgeous, she stood talking to a cluster of Morris people. The short dress revealed her long, shapely legs and he could take a slow look now when she was unaware of his gaze on her. Her hair was looped and piled on her head, but this time a few strands escaped to frame her face.

She laughed at something someone said and his heart jumped. Instantly a vivid memory of Jessie Smith struck him.

His gaze narrowed while he focused intently on Isabelle, looking slowly, trying to compare her to a memory.

"Mr. Morris. I see your graphic arts department director, Isabelle Smith. Is that her full name?"

"As far as I know," Seymour answered, turning to the man at his side with a questioning look.

Tony's gaze remained riveted on Isabelle. He wanted to excuse himself and go talk to her, but that was impossible.

"It's *Jessica* Isabelle Smith," the vice president answered.

"Jessica Smith," Tony whispered, repeating the name. Jessie Smith. It *was* her. Jessie Smith was back in his life.

He couldn't keep from smiling. His new acquisition had a surprising, incredible perk. Now he could think of two reasons for her coolness when they had met Tuesday night. She could resent that he had not contacted her after their night together. Or she didn't want to recall that night or rekindle the friendship. He watched her, remembering the college girl he had met, taunted by a visual picture of a laughing blonde, stunning in tight, faded jeans that molded to her slim legs. The same riveting blue eyes and flawless skin. A mouth to elicit erotic fantasies. And a cascade of long, almost waist length, silky, pale blond hair that, instead of being tightly pinned and conservative, tumbled freely over her shoulders. A party girl. Fun-loving, flirty with him, burning him to cinders in bed.

Why had she switched to her middle name, Isabelle? Nearly everything about her had changed, with the exception of her gorgeous looks, her captivating blue eyes, silky blond hair and that blazing attraction. Tony recalled her in his arms that night, warm, naked, eager. She had been all the things then that she had not been when he encountered her Tuesday night—the night they had met, there had never been a barrier around her.

She must have remembered him from the start. Was she angry he hadn't pursued her after that night of passion?

Barely aware of his surroundings or the looming task, Tony's attention kept returning to her while he attempted to chat politely with Seymour.

Finally, one of Seymour's vice presidents quieted the room, introduced Seymour Morris and turned the microphone over to him.

Smiling his way through the opening, Tony heard none of it. His gaze kept resting on Isabelle, who was now facing the speaker, keeping her gaze firmly on the vice president or on Seymour. During the time Tony had watched her, not once had she looked at him.

He heard Seymour announce his name, introducing him as the new CEO and head of Ryder Enterprises, and he smiled during the applause. As he stepped to the microphone, shook Seymour's hand and looked around the audience, his gaze rested on Isabelle. This time he made eye contact.

The instant they looked into each other's eyes, the air electrified. Erotic images from the past taunted him as he pulled his attention back to the moment.

"I want to thank all of you for the warm welcome I've received. Seymour Morris and the Morris family have built a premier company with the help of outstanding employees. This is a blue-ribbon company with a blue-ribbon record." He waited a few seconds while there was polite applause.

"In the coming weeks I'll be talking to each of you more in depth. I think I already have appointments with most of you. If you need to see me sooner than your appointment, just let my secretary know. I'm looking forward to a banner year for Morris. I'll turn this over to my executive president, Jason Hoyt, who has a few words to say and some introductions."

He stepped aside and once again barely heard introductions

until they went back to the Morris people and one by one, the vice presidents and then the directors were introduced.

They were scattered throughout the room and each person waved while they received brief applause. As each name was called, he looked carefully at the person, recalling the information he had received regarding them. Finally, he heard, "Isabelle Smith, director of the graphic arts department."

Smiling, she stepped forward to wave, her gaze never meeting his. It didn't matter. His heart jumped while he studied her intently again, remembering Jessie, comparing, feeling faint doubts that were fading each time he looked at her. Off and on he had thought about her, wondering where she was and what she was doing. At the time he had been working almost every waking minute and he hadn't wanted to get involved with a woman because business would have suffered. She was back in his life. Now he could better understand her anger over his not contacting her after their night of partying and making love. Also, he could get through that barrier she had thrown up. As they made the next announcement, she glanced at him.

Certain she was Jessie Smith, he was jubilant.

The minute they finished the introductions and speeches, Tony turned to Seymour to offer his hand. "Thank you, sir. I have high hopes for Morris."

"I think you'll do well. This has been a great company. I have to tell you, there are moments this retirement gets to me, but I have no Morris heirs to pass this on to, so this is the end of the line. Life is filled with changes. I hope you pass this company through as many generations of Ryders as we have had Morrises."

"Thank you. You've built a great company and I'm looking forward to my involvement in it."

Seymour grinned. "Your father wanted this company in the worst way. I've fought him off for years. Lucky for you that you happened along when I wanted to retire and it didn't hurt that you had a better offer than your dad," Seymour added, chuckling. "Even though he didn't make the sale, I know he's probably still celebrating since you have a family business the same as I do. He may be out of it, but it was his and it's still Ryder."

"That he is. Best wishes on your retirement," Tony said, anxious to get through the formalities.

When he had the chance, he turned to look for Isabelle. Once again, he couldn't spot her. While his pulse drummed, he began to move around the room and then he saw her near the door, talking to three people. With her coat in hand, he suspected that she had been on her way out when someone had stopped her.

He tried to avoid rushing, but he crossed the room, putting off conversations with people who approached him.

And then she turned and walked out the door.

He lengthened his stride to catch up with her in the hall. "Jessie," he said.

Isabelle stopped, her heart lurching. *He remembers* was the first thought that went through her mind. Her palms became damp as she turned to watch him approach. Looking like an ad for expensive men's clothing in his charcoal suit, Tony had a commanding presence that was different from the party guy she had met in college. The thick mat of unruly curls were the only hint of a less serious side to him, something beyond the driven, ambitious mogul whose entire focus seemed to be on acquiring an even larger fortune.

As he halted only inches in front of her, there was a warmth in his gaze that hadn't been present on Tuesday night. He gripped her arm lightly, his fingers barely holding her, yet it was a heated touch. "Let's go where we can talk and not be interrupted."

"I'm not sure we need to talk," she said. "You're my new employer. I'll see you sometimes at the office," she said, starting to put on her coat. He took it and held it out for her. As she slipped her arms into the sleeves, his hands brushed her shoulders. The faint touch should have been impersonal but was scalding.

"Oh, no. You're not getting off that easily. Why didn't you tell me?"

She looked up at him as he walked beside her. "I didn't think you remembered," she said, her pulse racing.

"I've never forgotten. Tuesday night, I thought about you— the Jessie Smith I knew, but dismissed the idea because of your name, Isabelle, your appearance, which is far different. And your whole manner."

As they left the building, he held the door. "Let's go have a drink somewhere and we can talk."

She shook her head. "We're not taking up where we left off. Different time, different world. You're my new employer. End of discussion. I have other job offers, so soon I'll be leaving Morris."

"Don't act in haste," he said, his dark brown eyes unreadable. His handsome looks held her attention, more so now than when she was younger.

"I won't do anything rash. I've been interviewing, studying my options."

"Perhaps, but you haven't heard what we'll offer," he said.

"Frankly, I doubt it will top the offers I've received. And you'll have no difficulty replacing me, if you even want to with your ad department all in place. We both know that."

"Why not hear what we'll do? What do you have to lose?"

She smiled at him. "Nothing to lose. I'll listen at the office. There's no need for us to discuss work tonight."

"How about dinner tomorrow night?" he asked, and her heartbeat skipped. Acceptance was on the tip of her tongue. But she had had one foolish night with him. She didn't want another. Her aim was to meet someone with marriage potential— definitely not Tony Ryder's MO, he was not the settling-down type. She wanted marriage and family. Tony wanted success. Focusing on his workaholic drive, she could say no far more easily.

"Thank you. I have never thought it wise to mix business with my personal life. That's the path to all kinds of complications."

"I think you cut off your options too hastily," he said, smiling at her. "I'm still glad to find you again. I suppose it's Isabelle now and not Jessie."

"Definitely. Jessie was a nickname from childhood. My grandmother was named Isabelle and I loved her and always wished Isabelle had been my first name. When I graduated from college, I saw an opportunity to move into a different world with different friends and change to the name I like best. I prefer Isabelle and most of my coworkers don't even know Jessica, much less Jessie."

His gaze roamed over her features, his scrutiny making her breathless. "I hope you come to work sometime with your hair down. I remember your long hair," he said in a husky voice.

And I remember your broad shoulders and rock-hard body, she thought. "I don't wear my hair down to work," she answered in what she hoped was a remote voice. "It doesn't seem as professional."

"So when you knew I was coming, you began looking for another job?"

"Actually, the companies contacted me. I intended to look other places, and now I've had promising offers."

"You've said you'd wait and give us a chance."

"I will, but I'm pretty sure I'll be leaving and even more certain you'll never miss me." It was tempting for her to add, *You didn't before.* "I need to go. I told Mr. Morris goodbye. I'll miss him, but he seems happy with the prospect of retiring."

"I'll walk you to your car," Tony said, falling into step beside her. "Catch me up. Did you go from college to Morris?"

"No. I worked for an ad agency for two years and then came to work here."

At her car she stopped and smiled. "Good night," she said, pulling her coat close around her.

"Night, Isabelle. I'll see you at the office."

She slid behind the wheel. He closed the door and stepped back.

As she drove away across the parking lot, she glanced in the rearview mirror. He stood staring at her car.

She had turned down dinner and told him she was quitting. Exactly what she should have done, but there was part of her that wanted to accept his dinner offer and stay in his employ.

This had to be for the best. She didn't want any more nights of mindless liaisons, a brief casual relationship with her employer that meant nothing to him. She wanted out of this company and away from Tony Ryder with her heart and her self-respect intact. And she didn't want the office gossiping about her relationship with the new owner. Tony Ryder was not the person to get involved with and she regretted that he had recognized her. She intended to keep reminding herself that he was not the kind of man she wanted to spend her time with.

Even so, there was part of her that wanted to stay at Morris. A part of her that knew she would see more of Tony if he was her boss.

As she studied an ad layout at the office Friday morning, Isabelle received a call from Tony's secretary, who wanted to set up a meeting. Within minutes Isabelle had an eleven-o'clock appointment Monday with Tony, his president of operations and the president of promotion and information. She was still tempted to turn in a resignation and skip the interview, but she was curious how badly he wanted her to stay. What offer would he make?

She had already decided which company she would prefer

to join. She had had the third interview, which had culminated in a job offer that included more money than she was making. She would oversee a larger graphic arts department in an office with a more convenient location. She did not expect Tony to top their proposal, giving her the opportunity to tell him she had a better offer. Going with that thought firmly in mind, she spent the weekend getting ready for her business move, hoping to take off a few days in between employers. Saturday morning she went to a midmorning meeting of Dallas Regional Graphic Artists. She had belonged to the group since she had started her career.

As she expected, a close friend greeted her upon her arrival. Dylan Kinnaly—who was seriously involved with Tony's sister, Sydney—broke away from a cluster of people and hurried toward her. The tall, slender man had a worried frown that indicated something bad had happened.

"Have you met him yet?" Dylan asked. "You said Tony Ryder takes over now."

"Hello, to you," she answered with amusement. "Yes, I've met him. He wants me to stay with Morris."

"Sydney's parents had a long talk with her about me. I was hoping to talk with you when we get a chance. Can you stay after the meeting?"

"Sure, the room will be empty," she said, her curiosity rising. Dylan had become a good friend over the years and she had been surprised when she had learned he was seeing Tony's sister.

She had first met Sydney Ryder at an annual film festival held by one of the local art museums. Later, she had seen her a few times at professional events when Dylan had brought her along. She couldn't keep from liking Sydney and couldn't blame her for anything her brother did. But Sydney was a reminder of Tony, and for that reason Isabelle had refused the few invitations from Dylan to go to dinner with them. When she had told Dylan about meeting Tony in college, swearing him to secrecy about telling

Sydney, Dylan understood her refusal to get to know Sydney better.

"The meeting's beginning so we'll talk later."

They took seats and listened as a speaker took the podium. The meeting was short, lasting only an hour.

It wasn't until they were alone that Dylan turned to her. Since his blue eyes were clouded with worry, she braced for bad news. "Sydney called me last Tuesday night. Her parents gave her an ultimatum. If she doesn't drop me, they will disinherit her, stop paying for medical school for her and cut her out of family holidays."

"Dylan, I can't believe that. Why?" Isabelle asked, aghast and wondering about the tensions in Tony's family. "How can they interfere in your lives that way? Why would they?"

"I'm not *society*. They want her to marry one of the men she's known all her life. Also, they think I'm after her money."

"That's dreadful," Isabelle answered. "Sounds like something out of the eighteenth century."

"I don't want any of Sydney's money," he said, his long fingers turning his pen in his hand. "I don't want to hurt her, either. We've talked it over. As far as I'm concerned, I see only one solution—I ended our relationship. For her sake."

"That's even worse. Does she go along with your decision?"

"No. She wants us back together, but they're threatening too big a disaster for her. I don't want her going through anything so stressful over me. She's always loved her family and they've been close. She's very close with her brother."

"What's does Tony think of all this?"

"He said he would send her to medical school, not to worry about that one."

"Good for him," Isabelle said, relieved and aware of a grudging respect blossoming for Tony. "He can afford to do that. I was afraid he would side with his folks."

"Not at all. He gave her a generous check. He told her he

would never cut her out on holidays—or ever. He urged her to tell me their threats. Tony is damn supportive, but from what Sydney has told me, Tony has had bitter battles with his dad."

"I'm glad Tony took that stand," she said, her respect growing stronger. "I think more of him for not siding with them, and for urging her to tell you their threats."

"They may treat him the same way when he gets engaged if it isn't someone they approve of."

"Tony Ryder is a complete workaholic," Isabelle said. "I can't imagine him getting married. He won't have the same problem with his parents. I'm sorry, Dylan. If she truly loves you and you love her, maybe you should give it more thought before you break off with her."

"I just don't want to cause her to lose her inheritance—or her parents."

"She's in love with you. I understand your feelings, but think about it."

She gazed into eyes that were darker blue than her own. Dylan was a good graphic artist and they had helped each other in years past on projects. She hated to see him hurt and she thought the Ryders were being ghastly about him.

"What about you and Tony Ryder?" Dylan asked. "Have you seen him yet? Does he remember you?"

"Yes and yes. He remembers me and he wants me to stay with Ryder Enterprises."

"You're damn good at what you do. You've built that department. Will you?"

She shook her head. "The department will never be the same. I don't want to stay. There's no future with Tony."

"I don't blame you. If I could do it over—" He paused to think and shook his head. "I'd still want to know Sydney. I love her and you can't turn that off. Not the last-forever kind of love."

"Dylan, I'm so sorry. They should be delighted with you."

He smiled. "Thanks. I naively thought they would at least be riendly to me. They aren't even that. I'm not supposed to set oot in their house."

"This goes from bad to worse," she remarked. "What a family. Maybe you don't want to marry into it. Do you know Sydney really, really well?"

"I love her with all my heart. Enough to get out of her life and avoid causing her heartache."

"I'm sorry. I don't have a solution for you, except to urge you to rethink walking away from the woman you love and who loves you. Think about what's important. Think about what Sydney wants."

Dylan smiled briefly at her, and they got up to head out. As they walked toward the door, he said, "No one has a good solution, but thanks for listening. Be careful with Tony if he wants you to go out with him. You could end up in a dilemma with his family. Sydney said they have women picked out for him."

Isabelle laughed. "Don't worry. There's no danger. Tony Ryder is in love with his work. He's married to his job. I don't ever want to tie my life to someone who puts work first over family. I saw that happen with one of my friend's family when I was growing up and it was dreadful.

"True love is a precious thing. Think about it, Dylan, before you do something drastic."

"I'm thinking, but I always come back to the same solution. I love her and want what's best for her."

"I hope she appreciates the kind of person you are. It sounds as if she does. Don't rush into a breakup, Dylan. That's my two cents' worth."

"That's why I wanted to talk to you about this."

"Keep in touch and let me know what's happening," she said, going to her car as Dylan headed to his.

"You do the same," he called, walking backward. "If you change jobs, please let me know."

"I will," she called, climbing into her car, moving by rote while she thought about what she had learned from Dylan. She didn't want to be involved with Tony in any manner.

One more strike against getting to know Tony Ryder any better. His family would be no more happy with her than they were with Dylan. At least Tony had stood by his sister. Isabelle had to admire him for that.

Sunday afternoon, she looked at her wardrobe to select what she would wear to the Monday interview. Certain she would soon leave Morris, she decided to wear something both professional and a little less buttoned up than usual, something more on the appealing side. Her conservative suits were shades of blue, gray, brown and black, innocuous, all business, hopefully authoritative to offset her age and pale blond hair. Although she was five feet eight inches tall, she wore high heels. She rummaged through her choices, pushing aside the suits to withdraw three dresses, which she tried on in succession.

Tony had forgotten her before and he would again, but she wanted him to notice her Monday and remember her after she was gone from his company. She had to stop thinking of it as Morris and recognize that it was now Ryder Enterprises, a name that gave her a bitter feeling because of Tony and their past, as well as having loved the Morris company the way it had been. Mentally, she had mapped out a rosy future with Morris and then Tony Ryder had brought it crashing down. Unfair a little, because Mr. Morris was also responsible by retiring and selling out.

She finally decided on a deep blue dress with a short jacket and a straight skirt that had a slit on one side. The low-cut square neckline revealed curves while the whole dress clung to her figure. She had matching pumps that would complete her ensemble. Eager to resign and move on with her life, she looked forward to the interview.

* * *

Monday morning she was ushered into the elegant office that had always belonged to a Morris. The thick carpet muffled any footsteps while the early morning sun poured through the floor-to-ceiling windows, spilling across the balcony and into the room. She imagined a smiling Mr. Morris sitting at his broad mahogany desk. Instead, it was Tony, vibrant, commanding, sexy enough to transform what was usually a purely business atmosphere into an electrified ambience. Smiling, he stood, coming around his desk to greet her while another man remained beside a leather chair. A brunette who had been sitting nearby stood.

"Good morning, Isabelle," Tony said, taking her hand to shake it briefly. The moment they touched, her already racing pulse gave another spurt. She withdrew her hand swiftly. His brown eyes were friendly. Unruly black locks curled on his forehead, an unwanted reminder of being in his arms and combing them back from his face.

Instantly, she tried to concentrate on the interview ahead, but when she met Tony's gaze, there was a mocking look, as if he knew exactly what she had been thinking.

He could not possibly know, yet her cheeks grew hot and she turned from him to greet the others.

"This is Mandy Truegood, president of public relations and media promotion," Tony said as the brunette smiled, extending her hand.

"And this is Porter Haswell, our president of operations."

The man smiled, shaking her hand. While he was friendly, his gray eyes assessed her. "I've heard good things about you, Isabelle. It's a pleasure to meet you. I never did get to talk to you at the reception, which I had intended to do."

"Sorry I missed you," she replied. "I left early," she added, without a glance at Tony.

"You've had a spectacular career with Morris, with many awards. Congratulations," Porter said.

"Thank you," she answered. "Morris gave me opportunities. They opened the new hotel chain just shortly before I started, so from the beginning I got to do the ad campaigns. This is a great department with a talented staff. You'll find each person brings a particular specialty. The teamwork is amazing."

"You can tell us about your staff. Why don't we have a seat. We can sit at the conference table," Tony said.

She moved to the rectangular table. Effortlessly, Tony was there before her, pulling out a chair for her.

"Thanks," she said brusquely as he sat to her right. She marveled how he could appear both relaxed and in control at the same time, a puzzling combination. On the table was her own large portfolio, plus a file bearing her name.

Amanda and Porter placed notebooks and papers in front of their seats.

Tony gazed at her with a faint smile. "We've studied your portfolio and impressive file that lists your accomplishments and awards."

"I look forward to working with you," Amanda added. "Morris is a great company and you've contributed to its growth."

"Why don't you tell us about the campaign that you feel you contributed to the most and how you worked with your staff," Tony suggested.

As she talked, she was aware of holding the attention of all three, Amanda asking the most questions, Tony's dark eyes on her while he listened.

The interview went easily. Isabelle tried to inform them of the talent and abilities of her staff. Even though she intended to move on, she hoped they kept her people.

When they concluded, remarks were brief, thanks exchanged

and she left Tony's office, the office she would forever think of as Mr. Morris's.

Relieved to have the interview behind her, and curious what they would offer, she went to her office to clean out her desk. It would be a simple matter to pack her things after she turned in her resignation.

She already had a resignation letter written and copies made, but she wanted to wait and see what Tony offered. She expected far less than she had now. He had a reputation for buying companies, gutting them and keeping only skeleton crews that he moved down the corporate ladder. Some stayed and moved back up in a short time. Most left.

She had no intention of working with him. Their night of passion was a shadow hanging over her, something she had not been able to forget. She suspected from his dinner invitation that he wanted to renew the intimacy. She wanted to bury the memory, but there was no way she could wipe it out.

Her phone rang and she was caught up in business the remainder of the morning.

It was after three when Tony's secretary called to ask her to come to Tony's office. Relieved they were doing something today, Isabelle hurried along the hall to the large corner office Tony occupied. All she had to do was give two weeks' notice and she would be elsewhere, far from Tony Ryder.

Three

When she entered his office, Tony stood in front of his desk, motioning her to a chair. His gaze swept briefly over her, a look that from anyone else would have been impersonal, unnoticed, but when Tony studied her, she warmed beneath his gaze.

He still appeared as if ready for a men's fashion shoot in a navy suit that had no wrinkles and his fresh snow-white dress shirt.

"Please be seated," he said, the words harmless, the look in his eyes not. His dark eyes smoldered with blatant lust.

Aware of his continued scrutiny as he sat facing her, she sat and crossed her legs.

"You had a good interview and made quite an impression this morning." He leaned forward, placing his elbows on his knees. "While I suspect you already have one foot out the door, I want you to stay and work for me."

"I have some very good offers."

"We'll top them," he replied without hesitation. "Here's what I'm offering." He stretched his arm to pick up a sheet of paper from his desk to hand to her.

As she swiftly scanned a neatly typed page with spaces filled in by Tony, her breath caught. She glanced up at him in amazement.

She looked again at the title, reading it aloud, "Vice President of Graphic Arts." She skimmed down the page to the salary that took her breath again. It was higher than any amount she had ever made, higher than what she had been offered by anyone. Shocked, she looked up at him. "You'll raise my salary this much? You would put me over your people?"

"You're good at your job. Seymour Morris praised you highly. You have an impressive record. In addition, you had a good interview. I want to keep you and I think to do so will take a bigger salary. My guess is that you are on the verge of accepting one of those offers you've received, if you haven't already done so."

"You're right," she admitted, looking again at the amount, far more than she could hope to make anywhere else. Too much to resign and walk away without consideration. Too much to even have to think long about it. The title in itself was a promotion. How much had his offer been inspired by her work and awards— and how much because of his memory of their night together and wanting to repeat it? She stared at the figures before her and the title, wondering about his motives. This was not in character with what had been rumored about his ruthless reputation when he took over a company.

"Do you want me in your organization or in your bed, Tony?" she asked bluntly, and one corner of his mouth lifted in a slight smile.

He reached across the narrow space between them to take her hand. Distracting, charismatic, sexy, Tony ignited a fire within her while his brown eyes held her gaze.

"You get to the point. I want to see you outside the office. I want you here in my company. Of course, I want you in my bed,

Isabelle. I haven't forgotten that night with you and you haven't forgotten it, either."

How she wished she could give him a long, cold stare and convey the impression of that night being insignificant and no longer in her memory. She couldn't possibly, which he was fully aware of. "I don't want to rekindle anything. On that front, you'll be incredibly disappointed if I take this offer."

"No, I won't. If you stay, you'll do a good job. I know that much from your past performance."

"I don't socialize, go out with, date, anyone from work. It prevents complications in my life."

"We'll see," he said, running his thumb back and forth on her knuckles. She pulled her hand away.

"If I thought you didn't like that, I wouldn't do it, but I can see the look in your eyes. I can feel your racing pulse. You react as much as I do and we *will* go out together. I'll hold you in my arms while I kiss you again."

"Stop that," she said breathlessly, the command sounding more an invitation than a rejection. "Tony, I'll have to give it some thought. I never expected this offer. As for socializing, even if we do, which we will not, won't that cause difficulty with other employees?"

"This is a private company. I own it. I have a good relationship with my employees. They are a happy bunch in a big corporation. I have married couples working for me. They socialize, eat dinners and lunches together. There are couples working here who go out together. I'm allowed to have a life. So are you."

"It won't be together."

"You're one challenge after another, Isabelle."

"I don't intend to be anything to you, not even your employee, although I may have to rethink that one."

"Let's have dinner tonight. Not a business dinner. It will be strictly social. Whether you stay or go, I'm going to ask you to go out with me."

She was tempted to accept his dinner invitation, except she could see her life tangling in a web woven by Tony until he lost interest. Socializing with Tony, an affair with him—not only would complicate her work life, but it would also be a path to heartbreak no matter how it ended. And it would end. When it did, she would be older with no family to show for her affair of the heart.

"Tony, if I accept your job offer, I will keep my private life separate from my professional life. Thank you, but no dinner tonight."

"Whatever you want," he said, smiling at her, sounding supremely self-confident. "I still hope you accept my job offer."

"It's flattering, tempting and amazing. I'd like to think it over and get back to you."

"Of course. Take your time," he said.

The moment she stood, he came to his feet to walk to the door with her.

At the door he reached out to hold the knob and block her from leaving. When she glanced up, he gazed back quietly. "I want you, Isabelle. We had an amazing night that I've never forgotten. You'll say yes sometime soon because you respond to me. You can't hide it. We both know you respond, just as I do to you."

With every word she was sinking deeper in desire. His seductive ways conjured up their magic. He was right on too many levels, his observations on target. If she stayed, it was simply a matter of time until she was in his bed. Was that what she wanted?

"Tony, that's the strongest of all the arguments for rejecting your offer," she replied.

"Scared how much you'll like your life in the future?"

He was *way* too confident.

"Wisdom says to shun meaningless affairs, as well as office affairs. The only way to do that is to avoid them in the first place."

"See, we could talk over an enticing lobster dinner or a thick steak tonight. We do have things to talk about. We could dance—as I recall, that was a great pastime with you."

"Sorry, no. I see no point. Thank you and I'll get back to you with my answer."

"Excellent," he said, holding the door for her.

She stopped to tell the graphic arts secretary that she was taking off the rest of the day. Gathering her things and the paper from Tony, she left to go home where she could think.

The following morning Isabelle stood in Tony's office again. She had dressed carefully, this time in a conservative tan suit and matching blouse.

"Please sit, Isabelle," he said.

"This won't take long," she replied. "I'll accept your offer. You know I can't possibly refuse. I won't find another like it anywhere."

He smiled, the devilish smile that affected her heartbeat and breathing and was difficult to resist. "Good. You surely will let me take you out tonight and celebrate. An early dinner and then I'll deposit you home. This is a big day in your life." While his brown eyes danced with delight, he smiled at her.

On top of the promotion, his offer was tempting, but some things had not changed. She shook her head and opened her mouth to decline. He placed his finger on her lips. "Wait. I can see you digging in your heels. This is an offer worthy of a celebration. If we didn't have a past, and you accepted my job offer, you would agree to celebrate. You've agreed to work with me, so we're going to be together, Isabelle. We'll work together, we'll be in meetings together, lunches, dinners, conferences, hotels. Stop worrying about one night and one dinner. Celebrate your victory. And this is a victory for you. No seduction. Just dinner."

She inhaled deeply. He had a point. She was going to work with him. She thought of the few times she had been with Seymour Morris, purely business. She couldn't equate Tony with Mr. Morris, but she was going to be thrown with Tony sometimes by working for him.

"I can see the wheels turning," he said. "You'll sit home alone tonight otherwise, will you not? No fun there when you have a real triumph. Stop making a mountain out of a definite ant hill."

"You're persuasive. I'll have to give you that much." She thought about sitting home alone with this fabulous new position dazzling her. One dinner. Maybe she was blowing everything out of proportion. She should be able to have a dinner with him without succumbing to his charm. She couldn't keep from wanting to celebrate this new job. "Dinner it is," she said, wanting to add, *Seduction, it isn't,* but she knew he would stand by his word about that for tonight. She nodded. "Thank you, Tony."

"Excellent. How about I pick you up at your house at seven?"

"Which means you are leaving work early tonight," she said.

"For you and your celebration, definitely. I'm glad, Isabelle. You won't regret your choice."

"Are you always so sure of yourself, Tony?"

He smiled.

She picked up her briefcase. "Now I have to go to Human Resources and fill out paperwork. I've been told I'll keep my same office."

"Yes. You'll get to do it over. We're having them all redone. Soon you can make the selections of furniture, carpet, wall colors, everything."

"Actually, it's very much the way I like it now."

"That's your decision. Welcome to Ryder Enterprises, Incorporated," he said, extending his hand, shaking hers. The moment his hand closed around hers and heat warmed her from his touch, she wondered again if she could cope with working in close proximity to him. She had spent a sleepless night processing his offer. The job was fabulous, a dream position and salary so good it was worth working with Tony. She reminded herself of how little she'd seen of Mr. Morris over the years, yet, she knew Tony would be different. It was just too good an offer to turn down. She ought to be able to work around him without being constantly drawn to him. And he was a workaholic. He would move on to other concerns. He was a deal maker. He didn't sit in one office all the time. She didn't really expect to see much of him after the first few months when he was getting the company set up the way he wanted. Even that, he probably left to others.

Shaking off uneasiness, she withdrew her hand. His enthusiasm was contagious and she smiled at him.

"Thanks, Tony. I hope you're keeping most of my people."

"We'll have a meeting concerning that later this week."

"I'll see you tonight," she said, and left his office.

The day was busier than she had expected and she got home with only a little over half an hour to get ready for dinner.

Was she already making a mistake by going out with him? But she had made her career decision and had no intention of fretting about it. She wanted to celebrate and she had begun to feel ridiculous for making such an issue about avoiding him. She should be able to treat him the same as any other man, Mr. Morris, Dylan, anyone. Just go to dinner, keep a distance, stay composed and cool and Tony Ryder would move on soon and forget all about her. No flirting. No intense reactions. Dinner with a new boss. Nothing more.

After showering, she changed into a red dress with long sleeves and a V-neck. She fastened her hair on both sides, allowing it to fall loosely down her back. Finally she stepped into red high-heeled pumps.

On impulse, she picked up the phone and called Dylan to tell him about her promotion.

"Awesome! That is terrific, Isabelle," he said, his tone changing from enthusiastic to somber. "He remembered who you are and wants to go out with you."

"Yes, he did. Whatever his motive, I couldn't turn it down. It will give me a jump in the corporate world. Even if I just stay a few months, I can get a better job than I had."

"As you told me, think about it. Be careful. His family is also Sydney's family. They won't accept you."

She laughed. "Dylan, they won't have to. Ever. Whatever I do, Tony Ryder isn't going to propose marriage. He's wrapped up in making a bigger fortune. I'm just going to work for the man. Speaking of Sydney. How's it going between the two of you?"

"We're talking. She wants to get back together. I still think it would be supremely selfish of me, yet I keep discussing it with her."

"That ought to tell you something right there. You want to be with her."

"Hell, yes, I do, but I can't be the one to cost her a family split plus losing her inheritance."

"Dylan, stop and think. She's studying to be a doctor and you're successful in graphic arts. You can both live comfortably and well. Multimillions aren't a guarantee of happiness."

"I'm not going to be the one to take her away from her family. Those kind of bitter feelings sometimes last lifetimes and that would be terrible. She's been close to them." He was quiet for a moment, then said, "Want to go to dinner? We'll celebrate your job offer and I'll buy your dinner."

"I'd love to, but Tony asked me if I wanted to go to dinner to celebrate and I accepted. Had I known, Dylan, I would have turned him down. I thought I'd be sitting here by myself. And I didn't want to make such a big deal out of trying to avoid him."

"Ah, sorry I didn't talk to you sooner. Call me on a night you're free and we'll go."

When they hung up, she stared at the cell phone before she placed it on the dresser. She hated to see Dylan hurt and Sydney had seemed like a fine person. She wished she were having dinner with a friend instead of Tony. Isabelle thought about Tony supporting his sister. Perhaps family wasn't as far down his list of what was important as she had first thought. She shook her head. She'd better not fool herself on that one.

When the doorbell rang, her heart thudded. Impeccably dressed, Tony wore a dark topcoat and his charcoal suit with a red tie. Only the thick, unruly curls proclaimed a streak of wildness in the handsome corporate tycoon whose whole life was wrapped up in his work. That and the look in his eyes, indicating his approval as well as his longing, made her pulse beat faster.

"You look gorgeous," he said, taking her coat to hold it for her.

"Thank you," she answered. "I'm excited over my promotion, whatever motives you have behind it."

His smile broadened. "I want you in my company. I want us to work together. I've already told you, I want more than that, but we'll go slowly. Have you told your family? If I recall correctly, you have a large family."

"You really do remember me," she said as they headed toward a waiting black limo. "A limo, Tony?"

"Sure. It's easier."

A chauffeur held the door and she stepped into luxury. Tony shed his coat and asked if she wanted to wear hers.

"I'm comfortable," she said, looking at the fine leather and walnut trim of the interior, realizing what a difference there was between their lifestyles, something easier to forget at the office.

"This is beautiful and makes the evening seem even more

of a celebration—at least to me. You've been riding in limos all your life."

"I'm glad you like it. I didn't remember what you were majoring in when we met. After I recognized you, it came back to me that you were interested in graphic arts even back then."

"Yes. It's all I've ever wanted to do."

"If I had recalled that, I would have known you and Jessie were one and the same. I debated the possibility that you were Jessie and dismissed it. You're more sophisticated now. You've been far cooler, less receptive, not the party girl I recall from that night."

"Responsibilities. Also, some resentment over your buyout of Morris, something I can't help. They've been great to work for and I had a dream staff."

"Hopefully, you'll like your new life even better. I'll see what I can do," he said, his tone conveying a promise that sounded removed from work.

"I'll manage," she replied, thinking he had incredibly dark brown eyes, almost black now in the faint glow inside the limousine.

He touched a lock of her hair on her shoulder. It was a casual touch, yet it was as fiery as a caress and made her wonder whether she was tempting fate by going with him.

"You're decisive—another good trait," he said. "Simplifies life. It's always good to know exactly what you want to do."

"One trait we probably have in common," she answered, thinking she usually was decisive, but she hadn't been around Tony.

Tony's cell phone buzzed and he reached for it, giving her a nod. "Sorry, I better take it."

"Of course," she answered, turning to look at the scenery outside as they sped along the freeway. She heard Tony discussing a business problem with renovations on a hotel that wasn't connected with Morris, so she ceased paying attention to his conversation, surreptitiously studying him when his focus was elsewhere. If she could continue to appear as cool and composed the entire evening, she should be able to get through this dinner, perhaps making him lose a degree of interest in her. She would have a celebration of sorts if she could only ignore the man beside her, but that was impossible. She focused on the new title and job prospect, clinging to it, feeling a tingly excitement over her promotion and trying to ignore who had caused it and why. Finally he put away his phone and turned to her.

"Sorry for the interruption. Tell me, what's gone on in your life during the years between when we met and now?"

"Graduation, getting started in business, gaining experience at my job, making friends. What about you?"

"Mostly business. Nothing unusual. Have you told your family about your promotion?" he asked.

"No. Simply because I was late getting home from work and had to rush to get ready for tonight."

He was staring at her. "I like your hair. I like it best completely down—the way I remember it. Maybe before the evening is over."

"I doubt it," she said. "This is a partial concession. I rarely leave it down and unfastened. As for my family—I'll call them tomorrow night."

"Are they all here in Dallas?"

"Yes, as a matter of fact. Makes it easy for us to get together."

Shortly after, the limo turned into a private driveway, passing a pond with fountains as they drove to a canopied entrance with sparkling lights lending a festive atmosphere. She had heard about the restaurant, a famous one in the area, but beyond her means. Another reminder of the differences between her life and Tony's.

The door was held open for them and inside, the maître d' knew Tony, motioning them to follow as soon as they arrived. They were led to a cozy alcove with a fire burning in a fireplace and a view of the dance floor and stage where a small combo with a bass fiddle, a piano and drums played.

The table was covered in white linen with a bouquet of white gardenias floating in a crystal vase. She could detect the flowers' sweet scent, but her attention was held by the handsome man she was with. A candle highlighted Tony's prominent cheekbones, catching glints in his midnight curls.

A bottle of champagne on ice already waited and the sommelier appeared to uncork the Dom Pérignon. As soon as he received Tony's approval, he poured the pale, bubbly liquid into crystal flutes. Iced shrimp, a steaming artichoke dip and a plate of bruschetta were brought for appetizers. Menus were placed before them.

When they were alone, Tony raised his glass. "Here's to a fabulous promotion in your career and a night to celebrate."

"Thanks to you," she said, thinking he still made it sound as if work was the last thing on his mind even though he referred to her career.

"Actually, both Mandy and Porter were enthusiastic about you and deserve some of the credit for your job offer."

"That's nice to hear," she said, surprised. She had assumed the exorbitant raise and promotion had been all Tony's doing to keep her at Morris. "You can't tell me Mandy and Porter helped set the salary you'll pay me."

The corners of Tony's mouth raised slightly. "No, they didn't. I don't want to lose you. I go after what I want."

Her heartbeat fluttered in spite of the red flags of warning his statement raised. He had made his intentions clear and she hoped she was making hers just as clear, although accepting dinner tonight had to have sent a mixed signal. Though turning down a celebration of his fantastic offer would have been its own announcement of how much she reacted to him.

"Don't read too much into this dinner," she cautioned. "I'm celebrating with you, which frankly, is more of a celebration than sitting at home by myself tonight or worse, working late. As you said, it is not a monumental deal," she added, hoping she sounded casual about the whole evening with him.

He looked amused. "I'm glad you're here, whatever the reason. I want to get to know you."

"Try to keep an employer-employee view. That's all it will be between us. Unless of course, you decide to become a marrying man. I'm interested in marrying in my near future," she added, enjoying herself because she suspected he did not want to hear what she was telling him. She was not only telling him the truth, she was also hoping to make him realize they had no future together. She had no doubt that a woman looking for a husband was the last person Tony would want to spend time with.

"I'm not a marrying man. We can still enjoy an evening out," he replied smoothly, and she wished she could remain as cool as he was. "As a matter of fact, with your attitude, I'm surprised there's no wedding ring on your finger. I can't imagine there haven't been proposals."

"I've been far too busy. The right person has never come along. Where we differ— You don't want to be tied down for years. I do. I want a family, so our association outside of work isn't a good idea."

"We'll see about that one," he said, smiling at her. "I realize you know how to enjoy life. I have a memory."

"I'm older now and life changes," she said, sparring with him. "What are your goals, Tony?" she asked, hoping to change the conversation, which was taking a direction she didn't want.

"I have *a* goal—billionaire by forty."

"Unattainable for ninety-nine point nine percent of the world."

"I doubt if the odds are that bad. What about your main goal? Did your promotion bring you closer to achieving it?"

"No. I want to succeed and have a rewarding career, but I

want a family like the one I grew up in. I love my family. I hope to be married by thirty."

"Married by thirty. That's unique today. Your goal doesn't scare away most guys?"

She hoped it scared away Tony, which was why she was happy to continue bringing up the topic. "I don't tell my intentions to everyone. You may be the first to ask about my goals. You're business oriented."

"Not altogether," he said softly.

"Oh, yes, you are. Time will prove my case."

"Business wasn't my driving purpose the night we met. It's not tonight." She gazed into his dark eyes across the candlelight. In depths of brown was craving that kept her excitement simmering. "Forget business. Let's go dance once before dinner," he suggested.

He held her hand and she stepped into his arms for a ballad. She already knew he was a good dancer, remembering vividly being in his arms the night they met. He pulled her closer and they danced in perfect rhythm. In that moment she realized just how hard it would be to stay away from him in her new role. Besides his handsome looks, he had too much else going for him. He had made it clear he was not into marriage, family, children—commitment—because they would interfere with his focus on business. He had already mapped out his most important goal. If she didn't want heartbreak, she needed to continue to guard her heart.

"Why so quiet?"

"Thinking how strange it is to be dancing with my boss."

"Stop thinking of me as your boss. It's Tony—the Tony you met a long time ago. Forget the office. Enjoy the night."

"I'm enjoying every minute. A limo, champagne, candlelight, a handsome man."

"You're beginning to sound like the Jessie I remember.

I assume you no longer want to be called Jessie by anyone, including me."

"Maybe you most of all. I don't want to explain to anyone why you would call me Jessie."

"I won't until you approve, but I can't keep from thinking of you as Jessie."

He looked into her eyes and smiled. How easily she could fall into his bed. Beware, beware. When Tony spun her around and dipped, she had to cling to him, looking up into his riveting brown eyes. Electricity sparked between them, generating desire.

"You're beautiful, Isabelle," he whispered as he straightened up and they danced together. "I'm glad I bought out Morris. I never would have found you otherwise."

"Tony, let's keep this an impersonal friendship."

"Sure," he said, his expression telling her something else. When the ballad ended, they returned to their table.

After the waiter finished taking their orders, Tony asked, "Where do you go on vacations?"

"I don't take them much. Last summer I kept putting it off and suddenly the year was gone."

"We have to change that. When is the last time you left the country?"

"Tony, I'm tied up in work. I grew up in an ordinary, working-class, blue-collar family. I haven't been out of the country."

"Definitely has to change. When was the last time you left Texas?"

"I did go to a grand opening of one of the Morris hotels in Atlanta two years ago," she said, sipping her champagne. "Unless you've made changes, the company is sending me to a preview before the official opening of an elegant new Morris luxury hotel in San Diego the weekend after next," she said, wondering whether he already was aware of her trip.

"Excellent. San Diego is beautiful and I'm sure the hotel will be grand. What day do you leave?"

"Thursday morning. Three of us are going, two of the Morris vice presidents—Nancy Wrenthorp and George Franklin—and me. On Thursday night hotel officials will show us around. Friday, guests will arrive—mostly media, friends and families of some of the hotel officials. We'll fly out Sunday morning early."

"Do you have any time to yourself?"

"Yes, on Saturday. Friday, I have appointments with media representatives. Nancy and George will deal with hotel officials and look over the hotel and see if everything is ready and running smoothly."

"You should enjoy your trip."

The waiter appeared with their salads, crystal dishes holding greens and slices of tomatoes. Her appetite had diminished and she still felt excitement fizzing in her as steadily as the bubbles in her champagne.

It wasn't long before their lobster and steak entrées appeared, more than she could possibly eat, yet all of it looking delicious. Again, Tony's phone buzzed and she waved her hand dismissively.

"Take your call," she said, understanding that as CEO and owner of multiple companies he was on call all the time. She surreptitiously studied him until he put away his phone.

"I couldn't help overhearing you, Tony. There was a fire on an oil rig you own. I didn't know you had anything besides hotels and the trucking line."

"Ryder Enterprises incorporates a variety of businesses. The oil company is a small but profitable subsidiary."

"Do you need to go? It sounded serious."

"It's serious and costly, but thank heaven, no one was hurt and they're getting it under control already. No, I don't need to go. I just need to be kept informed."

She smiled. "No danger of that not happening." She wondered if years ago he would have gone dashing out. Every moment spent with him drew her back into memories and heightened the attraction to him.

They both ate little and when their dinners had been removed, Tony took her hand to dance again. She went eagerly, wanting to be close in his arms while reminding herself to avoid getting too involved.

They danced to another ballad, followed by a fast number. Tony's coat swung open and his dancing was sexy, bringing back more memories. When they returned to a slow song, he held her closer. "This is great, Isabelle. Thankfully, I've found you again."

"I was never more than a phone call away, Tony," she said, stirring the simmering anger over Tony's buyout of Morris and his not contacting her again. Her anger with him had lost intensity. There were moments now when he charmed her and she let go her past feelings.

"You're in my life now and I'm in yours and I intend to keep it that way," he said and her heartbeat quickened. He wrapped her in his arms and gazed at her, his attention shifting to her mouth and making her heart thud. He would try to kiss her tonight and she wanted him to, but that's a line she couldn't cross. He had been building to that all evening with his flirting, his dancing, his compliments, his casual contacts. Everything he said or did fanned flames between them, even though this was *supposed* to be just a dinner celebration regarding work. Not a big deal, she reminded herself.

Shortly after midnight she told him she should go home. Tony didn't try to persuade her to stay out later.

When the limo arrived at her condo, Tony walked her to the front door. His phone buzzed again. When he ignored it, she said. "Go ahead and take your call."

"I'll get it shortly. Not now. Give me your key and I'll get your door."

She handed him the key, watching as he unlocked and waited

for her to enter. Every second that ticked past heightened her worry. Her insides fluttered.

"Do you have an alarm?" he asked as he followed her inside and closed the door behind him.

She turned to switch off the alarm and then faced Tony. "It's off. This has been a wonderful evening that truly was a celebration," she said, looking up into dark eyes that kept her heart racing. Her words were polite, somewhat impersonal. She intended to keep it that way in spite of wanting to be in his arms, to kiss and be kissed again.

She held out her hand to give him an impersonal handshake. "Thank you, Tony."

"That won't do." He took her hand and pulled her toward him, reaching out to comb his fingers through her hair, carefully removing first one pin and then another. She felt the faint tugs against her scalp, which made her tingle. While her heart drummed, her gaze was locked with his.

"This is the way I remember you and like to see you—with your hair down. Preferably naked in my arms in bed."

"Tony, that night is definitely over and it was very long ago," she whispered, trying to hang on to common sense and avoid getting more entangled with him in spite of her racing heart.

"But unforgettable. You're a warm, passionate, beautiful woman, and extremely appealing." As he talked, he removed more pins and more of her long, blond hair fell freely across her shoulders until all strands were loose.

"Ah, Isabelle, you're gorgeous." He wound both hands in her hair and then his arms slipped around her waist and he drew her to him.

When he looked at her mouth, her lips parted and she was certain he could hear her thudding heart. "We're not ending this night on a handshake. Since I saw you at the reception and realized you were Jessie, I've wanted to kiss you."

"Tony, don't," she whispered, her heart beating wildly. The

moment she had intended to avoid was happening. While his arms tightened to draw her closer, he brushed his lips over hers, a faint touch, but it changed the entire evening. Sparks spun from his kiss, transforming a casual evening into something more, making her forget any handshake. Tony brushed her lips lightly again, then returned to cover her mouth with his.

Isabelle's insides clenched and heated. As his tongue went deep into her mouth, longing swept over her, demolishing worries, igniting fires and rekindling desire. Memories of a night long ago bombarded her. Wrapping her arm around his neck and an arm around his waist, she clung to him, pouring herself into the kiss.

His arms tightened around her. His kiss was even more devastating than she remembered. White-hot, melting, his kiss shook her. How could he be so incredibly sexy to kiss when she didn't want to be drawn to him? She was annoyed with him, determined to guard her heart, yet barriers were dropping away, disintegrating from the onslaught of pleasure.

She ran her fingers through the short hair at the back of his head and then moved her hand across his broad shoulder.

Passion mushroomed, shaking her, driving her to wild kisses that blanked out everything except Tony.

He raised his head. "I want you in my life, in my arms in my bed."

"Never," she whispered, her actions negating her words as she stood on tiptoe and pulled his head down again to kiss him. She felt starved for his kisses, as if no time had passed between that spring night with him and now. Remembering his lean, muscular body, his broad shoulders and hard masculinity, she longed for what she could not have. A night she thought she was beginning to forget poured back, vividly clear.

"Tony, we have to stop," she whispered, even though her actions denied her words as she pulled him close to continue kissing him.

"Why?" he responded before her lips were on his and they kissed again. Passion blazed, consuming protests and reason.

Tony's kisses were beyond dreams, building excitement with lightning speed.

Dimly, she thought she should tell him again to stop, but the notion was fleeting. Giving herself, taking all he gave, she kissed him. She thrust her hips against him, feeling his thick erection, knowing he wanted her and was ready.

Feeling lost in a dizzying spiral, she finally summoned her willpower and stopped. "Tony, that's it," she gasped. She struggled for breath while her heart pounded and her body was on fire for his hands and mouth and loving.

With half-lidded eyes, he gazed at her, brushing long locks of her hair back from her face.

"That got out of hand," she managed to say.

"Not really. We only kissed a few times."

It wasn't *only*. His kisses had been earthshaking, seductive.

He held her waist. "You're special, Isabelle."

Her heartbeat quickened yet more. Words to wrap around her heart and make it captive. "Tonight was a celebration, Tony. I had a wonderful time and thank you. I suppose I'll see you at the office this week."

"Not this week, because I leave town," he said, his fingers caressing her throat.

"Thanks and good night," she said softly, looking into eyes filled with yearning.

"It was a special evening," he said. He swept her into his arms and kissed her hard. Startled, for an instant she froze. It was only seconds, and then she returned his kiss until he released her, watching her intently with both satisfaction and need.

"Until later," he said quietly. He left, closing the door. The lock clicked in place. She looked out the window. Tony was already on his cell phone, his long legs carrying him swiftly to the limo.

"You're a workaholic," she whispered, thinking about the calls he had received. The head of an empire, wanting to keep in touch with his business at all times.

In seconds the limo's red taillights disappeared around a curve in the driveway. She switched off the hall lights and stood in the darkened entryway. Her mouth was dry, and her body was on fire. She wanted him with an intensity that shocked her.

"Good night, Tony. Sexy man," she said, relishing memories of the evening. For the next few hours she was going to pretend Tony was just another guy she worked with and enjoy replaying the night in her mind. Tomorrow she could return to reality. The man was her employer. He was obsessed with work, chasing a goal of billionaire by forty. His true love was power. He would avoid commitment. She had to refuse his next invitation or kiss her own dreams and goals goodbye. She had to resist his kisses, resist him, remember to keep up her guard. Too much was at stake to get deeply involved with him. She promised herself she would hold her own goals always in sight.

At least until her next encounter with Tony.

Four

Tony entered the walnut-paneled study at his parents' mansion to greet his father, looking into brown eyes as dark as his own. It was a typical Sunday evening with a quiet house, the staff at a minimum, his mother at a friend's playing bridge. "You called and wanted to see me. What's up?"

"First, let me pour you a glass of wine. Have a seat."

"Make it a small amount," Tony said, not interested in wine, but aware it would please his father if he would sit and have a drink with him. Tony took a business call while Grant Ryder poured two goblets with white wine from a crystal decanter. He carried one to Tony, who replaced his phone. "How was the Morris party?"

"Fine. Everything went smoothly. I think the transition will be easy."

"You achieved the impossible, Tony, getting Morris to retire."

"I think he was ready and wanted to retire. I was in the right place at the right time."

"Don't be modest. It gets you nowhere." Grant sipped his drink and lowered his glass. "Where's your sister? Your mother and I haven't been able to get in touch with her and she hasn't returned our calls." Grant turned to face his son.

"I think Sydney is studying," Tony said.

"When did you last talk to her?"

"Yesterday, as a matter of fact."

"She has as much told me that she doesn't care what I threaten, she'll see who she wants to see," Grant said, his thick dark eyebrows emphasizing his frown. It always surprised Tony that he was over four inches taller than his father. When he was a child, he thought his father was extremely tall.

Tony nodded. "I'm not surprised."

"She's talked to you, hasn't she?"

"Yes. You know she usually does," he said, knowing from past experience his father was growing more angry. His words became clipped.

"Six months ago I would have urged you to try to persuade her to drop that Dylan person. Now I suspect it might be useless to try to ask you to do anything you don't want to do."

"You're right," Tony remarked with a faint smile, surprised his dad was even hinting at defeat in his attempts to control.

"So, it comes to that. I was afraid it might because you've always been strong-willed." His father sat in a chair and swirled his wine, looking at it for a long time before he sipped.

"Well, you've acquired sufficient wealth to ignore my influence in your life," Grant continued. "I could threaten to disinherit you as I have Sydney, but I'm afraid at this point, you would pay no heed. You'll do as you damn please because you don't need my money."

"That's right, Dad. It's worth every hour of work I put in," Tony admitted, relishing the feeling of being free from his father's attempts to dominate his life. He sat relaxed, enjoying the moment he had relished for years.

"You don't need to look so smug," Grant grumbled. He shook

his head. "I've met my match in my son. If I have to meet it, I can't think of anyone else I would prefer to best me."

"I wasn't trying to 'best you.' I just want to live the way I want to live."

"So what do you think of this artist, this Dylan 'someone' your sister thinks she is in love with?"

"First, my sister probably knows whether or not she is really in love with Dylan. Next, my opinion of Dylan—he's a nice guy. From all indications, he's good at what he does. What's more important, I trust Sydney's judgment, Dad. Dylan hasn't had the advantages I had or you had. Sydney is bright and sharp. Frankly, if I were you, I would trust Sydney's judgment."

"Love is blind, Tony. We don't want Sydney to ruin her life."

"Chances are, she won't."

"How do you know this fellow isn't after Sydney's money? Someday she will be immensely wealthy. That may be his reason for showering his attention and affection on her. Have either of you considered that possibility?"

"Again, I trust her judgment. Besides, Dylan has told her he doesn't want to ruin her life, so he doesn't think they should see each other anymore. He's sticking by that and he wants to cut all ties. Sydney does not want him to. You'll have to admit that's someone who is putting Sydney first."

"Damn smoke screen. I doubt if he means it. It sounds good, but wait and both of you will see. My guess is that he will let her talk him into coming back into her life."

"Maybe," Tony said. "Time will tell on that one."

"I'm glad he's done this for now, but I don't expect it to last. She can't put herself through medical school," his father remarked dryly. "I do have leverage with her even if I don't with you."

"No, Sydney can't put herself through school, but I can help her," Tony said, savoring the moment. His father's head whipped around and his eyes narrowed.

"Damnation. You've already told her you would, haven't you?" He didn't wait for an answer. "So you nullified one of my immediate threats."

"Yes, I did, because I love my sister. And I'm not cutting her out of my life. You and Mom can spend your holidays together as you see fit. I'll see Sydney."

"I never thought I'd see this day. I knew it was possible. Especially these last few years when you've had success after success. Dammit, Tony."

Tony smiled and sat in silence, still reveling in his triumph, recalling dreams as a boy of moments like this.

"So you'll help Sydney. Therefore, my threats are losing their punch. No wonder she's not taking my calls. Dammit, Tony," he repeated.

"If you try to cause Sydney trouble when she graduates—and I imagine you will—all you'll succeed in doing is driving her to move away. You'll lose her completely—and any grandchildren she might give you. She is already looking into where she can live when she finishes school. The places she's considering are far from here."

"I have to hand it to you. I'm impressed. I never thought I would see the day you could successfully tell me what to do and I would have to think about doing it."

"Learned how from you," Tony remarked casually. Silence fell and Tony sat swirling the glass of wine he had barely touched. He let his father ponder the transfer of power.

"Well, it's a new concept to think I might have to back off. You know it's a notion I don't like. Your mother may be another matter. She doesn't want this young man in our family."

"Does she want Sydney in our family?"

"Of course she does."

"I'll repeat—if you keep this up, you two will never know your grandchildren. You'll cut Sydney out of your life. Dad, for years to come, I have no intention of getting tied up in the demands of marriage, so don't think I'll give you grandchildren. You better make that clear to Mom."

A muscle worked in his father's jaw. He clenched his fists and walked to the window to stare outside. As silence filled the room, Tony recalled Isabelle informing him that her goal was to marry by thirty and have children. Her goal would have nothing to do with him except make her reluctant to have an affair, but he expected to get beyond that easily. And soon.

Finally Grant turned around. "You present a good argument. I don't like it one damn bit, but I have to be proud of you. You've outfoxed me, Tony. I suppose I'll have to consider your suggestions. With your opposition, I assume I'll lose a lot if I keep Sydney from marrying this fellow."

"That's good news, Dad. Frankly, I think in years to come, the whole family will be much happier if you accept Sydney's choice."

"If this young man doesn't break Sydney's heart."

"If he does, she will have only herself to blame. Not you or Mom. I better go, but I'm glad you're at least listening. Sydney's your child. You two will really miss her if you go ahead with your threats."

"Even if I capitulate, I don't know that your mother will."

"She will if you talk her into it."

"Go celebrate your victory."

"It isn't a war, Dad," Tony said. "Sydney and I just want to live our own lives now. We're adults. It's time you let go a little."

"If you ever are a father, Tony, you'll understand."

"I hope to hell I learn to let go when any kids I might have reach adulthood, much less in their thirties," Tony said quietly, feeling the clash of wills. He saw the flash of fire in his father's eyes and red flooding his face. "Don't let thoughts of losing control cause your blood pressure to rise," Tony added. "Just let go a little and trust us to make good decisions. Sydney is plenty smart."

"This Dylan person knows nothing of how we live. No telling what kind of life he will give her. I hope you remember that when you look for a wife and get someone from your own kind of world."

"Dad, as far as Sydney is concerned, she has told you what she will do. I've told you no marriage for me for years. You and Mom have to decide what you'll do. We all live with our choices." Tony looked at his watch. "I've got to run. I'm meeting my friends for dinner."

Grant followed Tony across the room. "Think about Sydney, Tony. You may be helping your sister to lose a lot."

"Sure. I'll think about her." Tony left the room in long strides, already making a call by the time he reached the back door, thoughts of family forgotten as he talked to one of his vice presidents about the coming trip.

After he finished his call and drove away, images of Isabelle returned. What was she doing now? He was tempted to contact her, but he expected another business call soon. When he talked to Isabelle, he didn't want interruptions. He called his pilot to arrange to fly to San Diego next Friday. He would surprise Isabelle Friday evening. Next weekend couldn't come too soon.

Twenty minutes later he entered the country club where his family had had a membership since the club's founding. Crossing the thick red carpet in the darkened bar, he joined his closest friends, men he had known from childhood, Jake Benton and Nick Rafford, who greeted him. "Where's your brother?" he asked Jake.

"Gabe should be here any minute. We might as well get our table," Jake said as the two shook hands briefly.

Tony turned to Nick. "Thanks for coming. I know this takes you away from Michael and Emily, as well as Grace."

"Actually, Emily fell asleep early, and Michael will soon. With the kids asleep, my wife will probably be happy for some solitude."

It still surprised Tony that Nick and Jake were married. They had been as committed to bachelorhood as he was. Both men seemed wildly in love and happy with their wives. Nick amazed him the most because he now had two small children. He thought well of Grace, but he saw no plans for any kind of serious commitment in his own life.

As soon as they were seated at a large, linen-covered table, Nick reached into his blazer pocket. "I know you're a confirmed bachelor, Tony, and you're a newlywed, Jake, but you're both going to see Michael's and Emily's latest pictures."

As pictures were passed around of his toddler girl and son, who was almost two, Gabe Benton walked up to join them, sitting across from his older brother with the family resemblance showing in the firm jaws, straight noses, thick brown hair and startling blue eyes. Gabe stood out from the others because he was the only one wearing Western hand-tooled boots with his slacks and dress shirt. All of them paused when a waiter arrived to take their drink orders. As soon as they each had a glass of wine, Tony raised his. The others gave him their attention. "You look like the cat that ate the mouse," Nick remarked to Tony.

"I've already made arrangements with the maître d'," Tony stated. "This dinner goes on my account. We're celebrating because now we have all ended our controlling fathers' manipulations. Nick, you have because you gave your dad the grandchildren he wanted. Jake, you have because you married and settled, and Gabe, you have the good fortune to have escaped, thanks to your older brother."

"Amen to that," Jake said as he exchanged a look with Gabe, who grinned.

"So what's happened with you?" Nick asked Tony. "You just said all of us."

"That's right. I'm including myself. Dad has admitted he has to stop interfering with me," Tony said.

There was mild applause and low cheers. "I'm set to make

more money than he has—in short, I don't need his money, so I can do as I please and he has no leverage to use on me. Tonight he admitted it."

"Congratulations!" Gabe and Jake said together, as Nick reached out to high-five Tony.

"Way to go, Tony!" Nick said, raising his goblet. "Here's to freedom from interfering fathers."

"We'll all drink to that one," Jake remarked dryly. "Mine threatening to disinherit me if I didn't marry—that is the biggest interference of all."

Nick lowered his drink. "I think Tony's dinner should be on us." He paused while Gabe and Jake agreed. "We want to treat you because you've earned it. That's tremendous. Something the three of us have wanted since we were about nine years old."

"Younger than that," Tony remarked and the discussion momentarily ended while the white-coated waiter took their dinner orders.

"I figured we'd celebrate your acquisition of Morris. That's probably what turned the tables with your dad," Gabe said.

"He realizes he no longer has any hold. He can suggest, but not threaten. Unfortunately, now he's focused on my sister."

"Don't tell me that," Gabe said. "Our dad has always concentrated on Jake. I hope he doesn't switch to me. So far, he hasn't."

"I don't think he will," Jake stated. "No habit established. Your investments are going so well, Dad has to be impressed."

"I've never said a word to him about them," Gabe replied.

"I have," Jake said. "I've told him you're handling my personal investments and some friends' investments."

"That probably shocked him."

"Besides, you're the baby and they've always spoiled you," Jake said with good nature, and Gabe's smile widened.

"Don't think I haven't enjoyed it, brother," he said, and the others laughed.

"Will Morris pan out like you expected?" Jake asked Tony.

"Far better," Tony replied, thinking about Isabelle and wanting to cut the dinner short and call her. Tossed green salads were placed in front of them.

While they ate, Nick lowered his glass of water. "This is a monumental day. A time we've dreamed about and I began to never expect to have happen. I insist you let this dinner be on us," Nick continued. "You've accomplished the miracle with your dad and you recently hosted us at a tropical retreat because of the bet you won as the last holdout for marriage." Nick glanced at Gabe. "You would never even enter the bet, so your bachelorhood doesn't count."

"I know that. I didn't want any part of the bet."

"My tag-along brother won't think about marriage," Jake remarked.

"I have no regrets about my lack of participating in the bet," Gabe said.

"Besides, Gabe, you would have had a distinct advantage since you are younger than the rest of us."

"We insist, Tony, on buying dinner," Jake added. "Since we were little kids, all of us have dreamed and schemed to rein in our control freak fathers and we've finally succeeded."

"Thanks. It's a great feeling to finally get free and to best him. Don't ever put Michael in competition with you, Nick," Tony said, thinking about Nick's son.

"Don't worry," Nick said. "I don't think any of us will ever do that to our sons."

"Or daughters," Tony added with his own sister in mind.

All agreed. After dinner they left the dining room to go to a club lounge, where they sat and talked until ten. Finally, it was time to head home. Nick was parked the nearest to Tony and before they parted he turned to clasp Tony on the shoulder. "Congrats, again. I never thought we'd see this day come for all of us. When we were kids we never thought it would happen."

"I enjoyed myself tonight. Maybe a little guilty for doing so, but damn, it was satisfying to hear my father admit he couldn't try to run my life any longer."

"I know it was. With Jake and with me, it all ended peacefully—at least I assume it's ended. I feel sure my dad won't ever interfere again. Besides getting older, he's wound up in Michael and Emily, the grandkids he finally decided he wanted. Who knows with Jake and Gabe? You're in the clear now. Sorry your sister isn't."

"I hate it. I'll pay for medical school for Sydney and I'll see her on holidays, but I can't do anything if Dad goes ahead with his threat to cut her out of his will. I can share what I get, but she'll fight taking it."

"Don't worry about it now. Your dad may change. My life with my dad is so different. Sometimes I can't believe he's the same man."

"Actually, my dad doesn't give up easily. I expect him to think about our conversation and come up with a new threat, but he knows he's lost any real leverage. If I help Sydney, I think he'll threaten to cut my inheritance. I won't be in the least surprised."

"That doesn't worry you?" Nick asked.

Tony shook his head. "I don't like losing a huge fortune, but I'll get along without his money and so will Sydney. He can do what he wants. I'm doing what I want."

Nick shook his head. "I admire you for deciding to stick by your sister no matter what. If it comes to losing your inheritance, let her know what you're sacrificing."

"The realization that I'm free to live my life the way I want to is like freedom to someone who has been imprisoned for a lifetime. No way am I giving in to him. His fortune isn't worth yielding again."

"Maybe it will never come about. Gotta run. See you, Tony."

"Night, Nick. Thanks again for dinner. I really think all of you should have let me treat."

"Forget it. You earned it." While Nick walked to his car, Tony climbed into his.

Tony wanted to call Isabelle, but it was late. "To hell with it," he whispered, and pulled out his cell phone to make the call before driving. The minute he heard her voice, his pulse jumped. He wanted to be with her. Next weekend seemed eons away.

Isabelle planned to spend the week trying to finish projects carried over from Morris. Tony left town after the Monday morning staff meeting and she didn't expect to see him until the following Monday.

She worked until nine Monday before going home. To her surprise Tony called. Several times she started to end the call, but he would always draw her back into talking. In spite of her better judgment, he kept her on the phone for over an hour with his humorous stories about work and interesting conversation. When she finally ended the call, she stared at the phone, looked at her watch and shook her head. "Isabelle, you're losing it. Say no to him," she whispered in the empty room.

Tuesday night when she arrived home, she found a large heart-shaped basket with a mixed assortment of spring flowers on her doorstep. Smiling and shaking her head, she carried them inside to read a card that was simply signed, "Happy Valentine's, Tony."

He called a short while later. "Thank you for the gorgeous flowers."

"Happy Valentine's Day," he said. "Wish I could be there to take you out."

"I'll enjoy my flowers immensely."

"That isn't the reply I was hoping for."

"That's about as personal as it will get, Tony. We don't know each other all that well."

"I beg to differ," he said. "I remember clearly—"

"Stop right there," she said, laughing. "I walked into that one."

"I do wish I were there."

"I'm sure you could come home if you really wanted to," she said, amused because he owned the company and could get someone else to take his place. She glanced at her watch, remembering she was going to cut him short.

"You're right, probably. Maybe I micromanage. I hope to hell I don't though. My dad did enough of that when he ran the business before it passed on to me."

"Tony—" she said, starting to tell him goodbye.

"Tell me what you know about the new ad campaign that was started just before I stepped in. The one regarding the East Texas hotels."

She told him how the campaign was going, what her department had done. She was on familiar ground. Eventually talk shifted away from business and she listened to Tony as she kicked off her shoes and took down her hair.

"You can tell me all about the San Diego opening when I see you. That's a great town."

"I'm looking forward to it."

"Better than where I am in the frozen north. Now if I had you here to keep me warm—"

"Tony," she interrupted, smiling and feeling tingles in spite of trying to avoid them.

"I'm just telling you what's on my mind. It really isn't ad campaigns or hotels. I don't want you hanging up on me when I've waited all day to get to talk to you."

"I know better than that," she replied, remembering all the business calls he had taken the night they had been together. It was over an hour later when she finally ended the call. She stared at the phone a moment, thinking about him. She should firmly end the calls from him. Or even avoid them in the first place, because she had caller ID. She took the call tonight to thank him for the flowers he had sent. But once she was on the phone with him there was no hope of cutting it short, because he always talked her into listening or answering.

Flowers, phone calls, a terrific job so she would stay. Where was she headed with him?

Wednesday night Isabelle waited for her close friend, Jada Picard, a Morris attorney, for their plans to work out at their health club.

When Jada climbed into Isabelle's car, she shook short, straight black hair away from her face and turned gray eyes on Isabelle. "Sorry, I got delayed."

"It's fine. I did, too. I've just been in the car a minute or I would have driven to the door to pick you up."

"After the workout, let's go eat. You can pick the restaurant so we can also celebrate your new job with Ryder Enterprises. How was your dinner last week with our new boss?"

"I'll have to admit, it was a great evening."

"Now that he remembers who you are, I imagine you'll have more excellent evenings," Jada remarked.

"No, I won't." Isabelle stopped for a red light and glanced at her friend. "I'm not accepting another invitation from him. So far, he's been out of town and when he returns this weekend, I'm away on business in San Diego. I'm staying an extra day just to enjoy the city."

"You'll have a wonderful time. I love San Diego. When you return, I predict you'll go out with Tony again," Jada said.

"A relationship with Tony won't happen," Isabelle said, remembering his kisses and being held in his arms, not mentioning the flowers and phone calls.

"Sounds like it could easily happen."

Isabelle moved in traffic, keeping her eyes on the road. "No, it won't. He's not for me," she said, despite how she had been dazzled by his kiss and unable to forget him ever, still recalling the long-ago night in as vivid detail as the recent evening with him. "I just couldn't resist the invitation to celebrate and it was beginning to sound like a big deal if I refused to go out with him. Otherwise, it was nothing and I won't go out with him again," she stated, trying to convince herself that she could say no to him.

"Doesn't sound like 'nothing' to me," Jada remarked.

"He's not my type," she added. "Jada, we're both twenty-eight this year. We've both agreed we want marriage and a family. For me, the time has come. Our new boss definitely does not want marriage or a family to interfere with his ambition. He's already married to his work. Friday night he had calls all evening long."

"Calls are not a big deal. His not wanting to get married— there you may have a stumbling block."

"I promise you, the man's work comes far ahead of anything else in his life. He's every inch the workaholic. I don't ever want to tie my life to one of those. Growing up, I watched my best friend's dad live that way and her mom had to cope without him. He was practically a stranger to his family. That's not for me."

"Yeah, if you grew up around a workaholic, you know what it means."

"Lucy's dad never saw her at any of her games, at recitals, at anything. She had nicer things than I did and a fancier home, but she would have traded some of the comforts for having her father around. My family was really close and she saw that. She loved to come to our house and she told me that was one reason why."

"How sad," Jada said.

"The quality of life is important. Fortunately, Tony is supportive of his sister. Their parents are giving her grief over the man she's been seriously involved with. They don't think he's good enough for her. I've told you about him—my friend Dylan."

"I remember meeting Dylan. He's a nice guy with a good job. What kind of parents does Tony have? In spite of his looks and money, I'd say two strikes against Tony. A workaholic guy with a snobby family. Be careful."

"Don't worry. I've seen the last of evenings out with Tony Ryder."

"I'd still say to watch out. Sounds as if he might be a heartbreaker. He has the looks for it."

"That he does," Isabelle agreed, envisioning Tony's sexy dark brown eyes and his thick, curly hair. "Have you ever gotten your interview appointment with him?"

"Not yet, but I'm not anxious about it. I've got really good offers now," Jada said. "I won't mind moving on."

"That's the way I felt. Having a place to go makes the future look much rosier. I knew you would get some promising job offers," Isabelle said, turning into the fitness center parking lot. "I need this workout."

"So do I," Jada said, climbing out of the car and getting her things to walk inside with Isabelle.

Soon they were both running on treadmills and conversation was impossible. Then each moved on to other machines. After they had showered and dressed, they left to drive to an Italian restaurant.

In spite of the workout and Jada's company, Isabelle couldn't keep memories of Tony from distracting her.

After a leisurely dinner she dropped Jada off at the office parking lot, where Jada could get her own car.

"Thanks again, Jada. The dinner was delicious."

"Have a super time in San Diego. I'll see you next Monday. Bring back pictures."

"I intend to. I haven't had many trips."

Isabelle waited while Jada climbed into her car and then she drove home. As she unlocked her door, her cell phone rang. When she answered, she heard Tony's voice. With a racing heartbeat, she shook her head while she listened to him, even though each phone call involved her more deeply with him.

"How's my most beautiful vice president?"

"Tony! That is so politically incorrect," she chided with a smile.

"First of all, I'm talking to you. Secondly, this isn't a business call and you surely never considered it as such. Third, it's definitely the truth."

She laughed, unable to be annoyed or take the question seriously. "So for now this call is not one between an entrepreneur and his employee."

"Definitely not. A man calling a woman he wants to be with, take out, make love to…"

"Stop right there. You always move too fast," she complained breathlessly, imagining his dark eyes holding their seductive look, aware for this moment she had his full attention.

"Always? Is everything too fast?" he asked, changing her meaning and stirring memories of standing in his arms while he kissed her slowly and thoroughly. "I'll have to work on that one," he said as if talking to himself.

"You know not always and not everything," she replied, knowing she sounded even more breathless than before. "Sometimes I would describe you as slow and deliberate," she said in a sultry voice, drawing out her words and enjoying flirting with him in return, even though she knew better and even though he was far away and not as much a temptation.

She heard his intake of breath. "We *would* have hundreds of miles between us," he said in a thick, husky voice, echoing her thoughts.

"You began this," she replied sweetly. "Maybe we should talk about business. Or far more safe, end this call that I really never intended to take."

"Business is the last thing on my mind now," Tony replied. "I have appointments tomorrow or I'd fly home earlier. Unfortunately, I can't. Why wouldn't you take my call?"

"We're headed nowhere, Tony. This friendship should not be pursued for some basic reasons."

"A minute ago you were enjoying our conversation."

"It was nothing but harmless flirting that you started."

"Harmless is not a good description. You set me on fire."

"You brought it on yourself."

"I tried to call you earlier when I had a break in my meeting. I missed you."

"Sorry, I switched the phone to vibrate and had it in my purse. I worked out and then ate dinner with Jada, one of my friends from work. You probably don't know a lot of the people yet."

"I know some. Jada Picard, lawyer?"

"Right," she said, surprised and wondering how many of the employees he could identify and if he learned only the names of those he planned to retain.

"I'm glad you weren't working late again."

"You did," she reminded him.

"That's also different. If I can get out of here a little earlier tomorrow, I'm going to. Snow is predicted and I don't want to get snowed in."

"No danger on my Dallas to San Diego flight," she said. She kicked off her shoes and carried the phone to a favorite chair to sit and relax while she talked, taking her hair down and combing her fingers through it, promising herself she would end the talk in ten minutes as she glanced at her watch.

It was half-past twelve when she wondered why she couldn't bring herself to cut him short on his calls. Even though she wasn't seeing him, they were getting to know each other better with the long phone calls.

"Tony, I have to say good-night. I was only going to talk a few minutes. It's after midnight."

"So you're enjoying this call as much as I am. We have a great time together, Isabelle. Let me hear you admit it."

"Not now or tomorrow or anytime after that," she replied, laughing.

"Just wait, I'll prove it to you. Let me tell you how—"

"Good night," she interrupted and broke the connection, laughing again. "Unfortunately, Tony Ryder, you're right," she admitted to no one.

Before dawn Thursday she was at the airport, looking for her colleagues in the waiting area at the gate. Since joining Morris she had worked closely with Nancy and George and she looked forward to traveling with them.

It was easy to spot Nancy's red hair and tall George's thick, wheat-colored blond hair. As they waited for their flight to board, she listened to them talk about their kids, thinking about Tony's determination to avoid marriage, preferring his work to a family.

"Lucky you," George kidded her, "you slept peacefully last night while Nancy was up at three with one of hers and my Billy had a basketball game, then dinner, then homework which included a project he needed help with so I had four hours' sleep."

Isabelle smiled with them. "What was the trouble with Molly?"

"Nightmares. She's going through a stage," Nancy replied.

"That's one thing—it should be quiet in the hotel. Nancy and I have dreamed of the few hours we'll be the only one in our rooms and absolutely no demands after midnight," George said.

"Once we're free tonight, I'll bet both of you spend the evening calling home and talking to your families," Isabelle said, knowing they kept in close touch. Their smiles confirmed her statement.

"After a call home," Nancy said, "I'm taking a swim in the pool. We've seen a hundred pictures as they built the hotel and the pool looked gorgeous. Either of you want to join me, feel free to do so."

"I will," Isabelle said, thinking how much a swim would be welcome as a relief in her busy schedule.

While they flew, Isabelle went over appointments and

brochures, names of California people she would meet. When they came into San Diego she gazed eagerly at the blue ocean below. Her anticipation grew. She looked forward to this trip for several reasons, business and personal, thankful for the experience and excited to see the city, the hotel and the ocean.

It was an opulent hotel, with a glassed-in lobby that had glittering crystal chandeliers, a plush deep blue carpet and a waterfall that spilled into a pool made of black marble. They went to the VIP lobby to check in, then headed to their rooms.

She spent the rest of the day touring the hotel, meeting the hotel executives, attending a meeting with them and then having dinner and enjoying a reception that included some VIP guests from the area who got a preview before the next day's activities.

It was eleven when she returned to her suite from the pool. The luxurious suite opened onto its own beachfront. When Tony called, she settled in a chair on the deck, switching off the lights so she could see the whitecaps while they talked for the next two hours.

Later, in bed, she gazed into the darkness while she thought about seeing Tony again Monday. She fell asleep thinking about him and dreamed of him.

Friday, her schedule was booked and included a dinner with media people that ran until after nine. They finally broke up and people left the banquet room.

In her suite she changed to her swimsuit, slipping into a T-shirt, shorts and flip-flops. She headed up to the grand rooftop pool, stepping out onto a well-lit deck with a bar beyond the crystal blue pool. A man near the bar played a guitar, the music clear in the night air.

She put her things on a beach chair and slipped into the water. When she reached the opposite end she turned to see a man enter the area. Her heart missed beats as she paused breathlessly because Tony stood at the other end of the pool.

Five

She was shocked to see him. She watched as he walked along the side of the pool. Her gaze drifted over him, his broad, muscled chest covered with a mat of thick dark curls. His biceps bulged with muscles and his narrow strip of black swimsuit left the rest of him bare, reminding her too clearly of their night of love and his magnificent body.

Feeling hot even though she was in cool water, she continued her perusal. His legs were long, lean and muscled. When he reached the deep end, he jumped in to swim toward her. Her excitement heightened the closer he came until he stopped only inches away.

He combed his hair back with his fingers to get the curls away from his face. While he treaded water to stay afloat in the deep end, she held the side of the pool. Drops glistened on his broad shoulders and she was aware of every inch of him.

Even the spacious hotel pool seemed dominated by Tony, his dark gaze holding hers as if she were magnetized.

"This is a surprise," she said

"I intended it to be, although I didn't expect to find you in the pool."

"I love to swim, but get few chances. The pool is convenient, so I've been swimming both nights," she said, feeling giddy. "You flew here from Chicago?" she asked, still wondering if he had come to look at his newest hotel or if he had a more personal reason.

"By way of Dallas first," he said. "How was your day?"

"Successful. I think they'll have a terrific opening and between our publicity and the media interest, we should get dream coverage. If you came to talk to any of the media, they're scattered all over the hotel."

Tony smiled at her, his eyes dancing. "Isabelle, I didn't fly out here to talk to the media or the hotel people."

She drew another deep breath, finding the air had grown rarefied and she was having difficulty breathing. "You're not here for business?"

"No. That's handled by you and others. I don't have to."

"You may have wasted a trip," she said, seeing red flags of warning waving. He had circumvented her plan to avoid being with him again.

"I don't think so," he said. "We'll swim and then let's go have a drink. We can talk about it."

"Are you trying to complicate my life?" she asked.

"Not at all. You had planned a swim, so we'll swim. Want to race the length and back? You can call go."

Momentarily caught between consternation and excitement, she stared at him in silence until she realized he was waiting for an answer.

"I'll race you. Go," she said, splashing away from him and swimming with long strokes, aware he was beside her.

She relished the physical action, for a few moments trying to avoid thinking about the rest of the evening, yet she kept recalling the vision of him standing at the end of the pool, almost naked except for the strip of black, appealing, sexy, breathtaking.

She pushed herself while he was even with her until the return. Near the end of the pool she gave an extra spurt and beat him, bobbing up as he did.

"You win."

"You let me," she accused, smiling. "Do it again and stop holding back."

"I held back very little. You're a good swimmer. Especially if you haven't been swimming often this year."

"I haven't been in a pool since last July. Race again? For real?"

He smiled. "Sure. You call go."

"Go!" she exclaimed, plunging away from him and stretching herself. He stayed alongside her until they turned in the shallow end of the pool and headed back. Then he pulled away to win handily and wait for her while she swam up to him.

"You won easily as I expected. I concede. I suspect that last race was one of the few times you've allowed someone to beat you at something."

"You're saying I like to win," he said.

"Yes. You're competitive, perhaps controlling."

He hit the water with the palm of his hand, causing water to splash her. "Controlling—I don't want to be that. I've fought that all my life in my dad."

"All your life?" she asked, treading water. "Surely you exaggerate."

"Hardly," he remarked. "That's one thing that drives me to make money when I already have a fortune. If I have more than he does—or he sees I will have, he'll get off my back."

"I can't imagine," she said truthfully.

"It's getting to be less a problem," he said dismissively and she guessed he didn't care to discuss it further.

She broke away from him, swimming lazily, and he joined her as they swam leisurely together.

When she stopped, treading water, he faced her to slip his arm around her waist and pull her closer. Her heart thudded because he was warm, wet, touching in so many places, legs, arms. "Tony—"

"I missed you this week and I've wanted to see you," he said. His brown eyes were dark as night with desire in their depths. Her breathing became difficult again and her pulse raced as she placed her hands on his chest, feeling his heartbeat. She wanted to stop fighting him, to wrap her arms around his neck to kiss him. The attraction between them was mutual and strong, but she saw that as a swift road to disaster. Resistance to Tony was her only hope for avoiding entanglement, which meant heartbreak. Yet right now, she was captivated once again, unable to break away, too aware of his hands on her.

"I wasn't going to do this again," she whispered.

"You want to. I can see it in your eyes," he whispered. He leaned closer. Without thought, she turned her mouth up to him and then his lips were on hers, her mouth opening at the first hot touch of his tongue. Their bodies pressed more closely together and she could feel his hard muscles, his warmth, his masculinity.

Her heart pounded as she kissed him passionately, pouring herself into her kiss, letting go her resolutions. His warm fingers went beneath her swimsuit top, pushing it away as he cupped her breast in his large hand. His thumb played lightly over her nipple,

Pleasure, along with need, burst from his touch. Moaning with relish, she once again responded and gave herself to the moment. She ran one hand across his back, over his hard buttocks, down to his muscled thighs, remembering, discovering him all over again. Submerged in water couldn't cool her because his caresses kept her hot.

She let him for minutes and then wriggled back. "Tony, this isn't a private pool. There's a bar up here—"

"It's private now. I asked not to be disturbed. They're gone. This floor is closed except to us. The elevator is here and doesn't go again until I say so. We won't be disturbed."

She wasn't aware of her bikini top being removed, but she was conscious of his hands cupping both breasts, his thumbs playing with the small buds that were hard, responding to him. She moaned again with pleasure while sensations rippled from each caress. His hand pushed her legs apart and he stroked her inner thighs, his fingers moving beneath her suit to touch her intimately.

Clinging to him, she gasped, arching her back as she twisted against him. Her excitement soared. His thick rod pressed against her and she could feel his readiness.

It was an effort to summon the willpower to resist. "We have to stop. I don't want to cope with the complications this will bring," she said, gulping air.

He opened half-lidded eyes to study her while his hands on her waist raised her slightly out of the water. Her breasts were bare, her top gone. Just his heated gaze on her was a caress that made her ache for his loving.

He pulled her nearer. "Wrap your legs around me," he said in a husky voice. His mouth closed on her nipple with his tongue stroking her.

Wrapping her legs around his warm body, she sighed with pleasure while he lavished kisses on her breasts, first one and then the other.

As he lowered her and kissed her hard, his tongue went deep. She was drowning in passion and complications. She wanted him, yet it would mean disaster in her life and possibly her career.

"We have to stop now," she finally told him, swimming away from him and looking for her top. She found it floating at the edge of the pool. While she pulled it on with her back to him, he swam up to her to kiss her nape.

She turned to him. "Let's get out and go have that drink."

His dark eyes devoured her, making her heart hammer even when she tried to resist reaching for him. She was telling him one thing, wanting another badly.

"Sure," he said, turning to swim away to climb out on the other side of the pool.

Trying to remember the reasons she should withstand his appeal, she swam after him. Now she knew why she had succumbed so easily that college night. He had turned on the charm at the party, his later kisses and seduction impossible to resist.

He waited beside a lawn chair with a navy towel wrapped around his waist. She climbed out, aware of his steady gaze on her, knowing he was still aroused, ready for love and wanting her.

Every inch of her tingled and her pulse still raced. She pulled on a T-shirt and stepped into her shorts, conscious of Tony's fiery attention.

He embraced her. "I want you, but I know how eager and passionate you can be when you lose your reluctance. I'll wait because I want you that way, with no worries about consequences, wanting to love as much as I do. I remember our night together."

She suffered both relief and disappointment with his declaration. He kissed her again and she couldn't hold back. Even though she was on fire with need, she wasn't going to go into a relationship that could tear up her world. If only she could hold to that stance.

Later, she stopped him. "I want to dress and then I'll meet you for that drink."

"Let's go. I'll walk you to your suite and wait while you change. Unless I can help."

Her head snapped around and then she smiled, realizing he was teasing, perhaps trying to lighten the moment between them.

"You can go to my suite with me and wait, but I don't need your help. Or you can go change and I'll meet you."

He nodded, smiling at her, but his eyes still burned with longing, keeping the tension high. "Meet me in the lobby. How long?"

"Give me half an hour."

He nodded. They had reached her door and she unlocked it. He gazed at her with desire. "I'll see you in thirty minutes."

She closed the door and hurried to shower and dress while her thoughts spun. Still surprised that he had flown to San Diego just to see her, the past hour replayed in her thoughts. He wanted an affair. Physically, she wanted the same. She was attracted to him, more than to any other man she had known, yet Tony would be the most disastrous man to become entangled with no matter how she viewed their relationship or the scenarios she played out in her imagination. She wanted marriage. Tony didn't. Even without marriage, she didn't want to give her heart to a man whose deepest love was his work. A thorough workaholic, Tony was driven to make money. She didn't want any kind of intimate relationship with a man whose thoughts were on his work most of the time. A man whose work came first always. It was a simple situation, but a resolution wasn't easy.

As Isabelle stepped out of the shower, she continued to weigh her options. Have an affair, maybe he would fall in love. For over hundreds of years, how many women had fooled themselves with that reasoning?

She dried her hair and began to dress in a conservative navy blouse and slightly flared matching skirt.

An affair would put off chances of meeting someone who had marriage in mind. An affair with Tony would complicate her life at work. He didn't seem to think so, but he owned everything. It was his company. Even if he succumbed to marriage, he didn't want a family and she did and therein was the strongest reason of all to keep Tony out of her life.

There was no happy solution in a relationship with him except the satisfaction of lust.

Go have the drink, let him politely know his trip was for nothing and get him out of your life, she told herself. She gazed at her reflection in the mirror as she twisted her hair to clip it on top of her head. There would be no politely brushing aside a man as dynamic and determined as Tony. So far, she wasn't getting the message across to him at all.

She looked at herself, hoping she looked poised, cool, reserved. By this time Sunday night she would be back in Dallas and, hopefully, she and Tony *would* part ways except at work.

All the way to the lobby, she kept telling herself to keep their time together short and then go her separate way. Her lips still felt his kisses, as well as his hands on the rest of her. She couldn't forget and there was nothing easy about dealing with him. Right now, her heartbeat raced, because in minutes she would be with him again.

When she entered the lobby he was waiting. His knit shirt and chinos were casual. The look in his eyes was not. Passion was a flame still detectable.

Her heart jumped as she smiled at him. He took her arm to steer her toward the elevators.

"I'm still surprised you flew out here."

"I'd hoped you would be," he said as they went to a small bar on the ground floor of the hotel. A few couples danced to piano music. Tony found a table in a corner. After they had ordered drinks, he held her hand to dance.

The moment they touched, her heartbeat sped up. "This is better," Tony said, pulling her closer. "I've wanted you in my arms and I've waited all week. Isabelle, I've found you again and I don't want to let you go."

"You're going to have to let go," she said as she looked up at him, his words giving her a thrill even as she denied them. His face was shadowed because of the dim lighting, but she could see his expression was solemn.

"Don't say that when we have fire between us. More than that. The first night was magical. You can't deny it."

"No, but that night was long ago. There's no future between us. I don't want an affair and you don't want to get married. When you're talking marriage and children, Tony, then we can spend long evenings together, kiss, see if there really is more than lust between us."

"You're young, Isabelle. You don't have to settle down and become a mother yet. You have years ahead."

"I know what I want."

"You say that to me, but when you kiss me, you tell me something entirely different," he said. "You can't deny it."

She wanted him to kiss her right now. She was fighting herself as much as she was Tony. She stopped thinking and just danced with him, relishing being held and holding him close, moving with him, inhaling the scent of him, clean, soapy, an appealing aftershave, his fresh shirt. Her arm was on his shoulder, her hand at the back of his neck. The vision of him getting out of the pool, muscles rippling, added to her smoldering hunger.

The music changed to a fast rhythm and when she danced facing him, longing intensified. Every twist of his lean body, his heated expression and the sexy twists he made revved up her sensual responses. His impact on her was heightened by the dance and by his concentration on her, which made her feel wanted beyond measure. Black curls fell over his forehead, transforming his appearance from the shrewd all-business entrepreneur to a sexy man filled with a zest for life.

Prudence and wisdom faded, becoming dim voices, melting beneath a burning sun of desire that threatened to consume her caution.

He spun her around and when she turned to face him again, he took her hand to pull her close against him, pausing in the dance.

She couldn't breathe or think. Her heart pounded. Longing suffused her, bringing with it erotic images. Immobilized, she stood pressed against him, forgetting where they were or that anyone else was near. She heard only her pounding heart and, faintly in the background, music. Tony's dark eyes held her captured as completely as his arms around her.

His appeal caused barriers to crumble. She wanted him and it was impossible to stop her reaction.

They were on the dance floor, not moving, lost in each other and forgetting the world, Tony seeming to as much as she. She stepped away and he released her. The music ended and she moved farther from him, yet he still held her hand.

A tango commenced and Tony pulled her, placing his hand on her waist to dance.

She fell into step with him, watching him steadily as they moved across the floor to a dance she always found to be sensual, filled with sexy moves when shared with the right partner.

"You've done this before," he remarked.

"So have you," she said, realizing they were both at ease and familiar with a tango.

"Who taught you the tango?" he asked.

"More a where than a who. I took dance lessons the first two years I worked. I wanted the exercise. Growing up, I had always wanted dance lessons, but my family couldn't afford them. I got a book at the library and tried to teach myself. Actually, I didn't do too bad a job with it. Who taught you?" she asked lightly, curious who had been in his life before she knew him.

"When I was about eleven years old my folks sent me to a cotillion program where I was taught the tango, waltz, lots of dancing, etc. My friends all had to go and we learned manners, as if they were not drummed into me at home. Try placing books under your arms while you eat to learn to keep your elbows off the table. That one was at home. Anyway, it was long ago, like other things in my past, but definitely not forgotten."

His last remark referred to their meeting. He didn't have to say it because she knew from the change in his tone.

They stopped talking, giving themselves over to the dance and to gazing into each other's eyes.

The tango heightened her erotic fantasies. By the time the dance ended, lust was primal. Tony had beads of sweat on his forehead. "I think we came in here for a drink," she reminded him, not caring about the drink but wanting to stop the sexy dancing that heightened tension with each step she took.

"So we did," he said, wiping his forehead with his handkerchief. He took her arm and they returned to their table, where their drinks awaited.

In moments a waitress appeared to take their orders for appetizers. As soon as they were alone, he focused on her. "I've missed you and thought about you all week."

"Nothing is fair about this, Tony, including you and your flirting."

"Let's just enjoy the evening. I know you can. You're all bottled up, fighting yourself and your inclinations because of some imaginary calendar in your life."

"Are you through analyzing me?" she asked, becoming annoyed, wondering whether her irritation was directed at herself or at Tony.

Tony raised his martini. "Here's to finding you again, Isabelle."

Even though she had a spectacular raise and new position, she didn't want to drink to Tony finding her again, yet she raised her piña colada. "To the future, Tony."

They touched glasses and he watched her as she sipped.

"I know the Jessie I spent the evening with years ago is sitting across from me. I'm just trying to figure out how to get her back. I never did forget. I just let go."

"That doesn't matter now. The night you came to see the Morris building, my unfriendly manner was because you bought him out."

"I think in the new position you have, I've made amends regarding the buyout upheaval. As of tonight, your work here is done. You're staying an extra day. Let me show you around. There's no harm in that."

She smiled at him. "Hopeless, hopeless. Your arguments are persuasive. So are your hands and your eyes," she added in a softer voice, and saw him inhale deeply. "All right, Tony, I'd love to have you show me around. Against all better judgment, I'm going to get to know you up close and personal. You don't take no well, do you?"

"Depends on how much I want something," he said. "Also, cancel your plane trip home. You can tell Nancy and George. I'll take you back tomorrow night with me."

"You assume I would prefer this," she said, amused and giving him a look. She was sinking and losing her battle and it was her own fault. If only he weren't so appealing and trying so much to charm her.

One dark eyebrow arched. "You want to fly back commercially instead of with me on my private jet? That will hurt."

"No, I'm delighted to fly back with you. It's just your assumption that I will want to. I think you've had your way far too much in your life."

"I'll have to admit, you've been a big challenge, but an enticing, delightful one."

"Thank you, even though being a challenge to you was never my intention. I just want to move on with my life." She sipped the cool piña colada, aware he still held her hand and continued to brush her knuckles with his thumb. She should pull away, but his touch was casual and she was tired of picking tiny fights with him.

"I seem to be losing the battles, though," she said.

"Good. I'm glad you perceive it that way. And this is much better. Now I'm happy I flew here. For a moment there, I thought I would have to turn around and go back."

"I don't believe you considered giving up for even two seconds," she said, and one corner of his mouth raised in a crooked smile. "And you do move fast," she continued. "I'm flying home with you. You're holding my hand now, plus I'm spending my free time with you. I'd say you're getting your way on a steady basis. For someone I intended to get out of my life, you're pretty well in it."

He leaned closer over the small table.

"One thing that didn't happen that night we met—I didn't get to know you. I can start making up for that now. You're a swimmer and you like dancing and art. What else is in your life?"

As he leaned back again, he continued to hold her hand, stroking the inside of her wrist with his thumb, light strokes she tried to ignore. His fingers had their effect on her, continually fueling desire, a constant reminder of the physical attraction between them.

"I work out at a fitness center, but otherwise, my job takes up most of my time."

"I read your résumé, so I know you grew up in Dallas, went to Tech on scholarships, have a stellar scholastic record and were on the high school debate team."

She held his gaze. "Your facts are correct," she said, surprised he had delved into her background. "All that education was for a purpose. I grew up in a blue-collar family. My folks sacrificed for us. Mom sometimes worked two jobs. Dad sometimes did. From early on I planned to do better and get out of that struggle. I aimed for college from the time I was young. In some ways, I was also determined to succeed. Just not on your grand scale."

"I'd say you've already succeeded."

"I know a bit about you, too. Your history is in the media. Golden boy, born into wealth, old Texas family, on football teams, excellent grades, enormously successful on your own. Not exactly similar lives."

"They say opposites attract. In some ways we're opposites. There were some similarities, too. We both had goals and set out to achieve them."

She laughed. "I'd say we're opposites in almost every way except wanting to succeed at work. Even there, you're far more driven than I am. That is your be-all and end-all, your major focus."

"There are plenty of times my attention is not on business. Right now it's on a beautiful woman. I want to get to know you, make love to you, discover what you like. You'll be more than a memory in my life."

"That promises giant complications."

"But, oh, such delightful ones," he said in a husky voice.

"Tony, stop flirting. Just talk."

"Flirting is far more fun," he replied, and she shook her head.

"Tony—ordinary conversation. Unless you want this evening to end earlier. Tell me your favorite things that do not involve women or your work," she requested, thinking she would steer the conversation to safer, more bland topics.

"Afraid of flirting and where it will lead?"

"I'm just dying to hear you tell me some of your favorites and your preferences," she said in a mocking, exaggerated accent, making him smile.

"Favorites and not involving women or work. I'd have to dig deep there and go back in memory. Way back."

"Surely not," she replied, laughing at him. She sipped her drink while they talked and she lost all track of time with him. The night was forever even while it seemed to be going with the speed of light.

"There's a good song," he said, glancing at the dance floor,

which held a few couples who moved to a slow ballad. "Let'
dance."

On the dance floor when his arms circled her waist, he leane
close. "Put your arms around me," he whispered.

She wrapped her arms around his neck, barely moving a
they swayed to the music. She felt his hands in her hair and the
a lock tumbled free. Faint tugs against her scalp as other lock
tumbled around her shoulders. She knew there was no use tryin
to stop him and it wasn't that important. Finally it all fell freel
around her face.

When he leaned back to study her, he dropped the pins int
his pocket.

"There, that is infinitely better."

"Still changing things to suit yourself."

"Yes, because you're even more gorgeous with your hai
unpinned," he whispered in her ear again. He combed his finger
through her hair while he gazed at her with satisfaction. "There
If you had looked like this that first night in your office, I woul
have known. You're beautiful," he whispered. "You take m
breath when I look at you and remember loving you."

How would she ever continue to resist him? It didn't help t
have him constantly conjuring up memories of their night o
love.

He released her slightly and danced her around the floor.

His total attention, his charm and his flirting all combine
to create an illusion that work was not his driving focus
For tonight, he made her feel as if she were the center of hi
world, absolutely necessary for his happiness. How easily h
conveyed the conviction that she held his complete interest.
was flattering, mesmerizing, seductive. She tried to cling to th
knowledge that he was pursuing what he wanted tonight, bu
Monday, his thoughts would be on business and her importanc
to him would diminish. Beneath his onslaught of attentivenes
it was a losing struggle to stay grounded in reality.

"Holding you in my arms is perfect. I don't want to let you go," he said in a low, husky voice. "Admit you like this, Isabelle."

She opened her eyes to look up at him as they swayed to the music. "You know I do without hearing me say it," she said, and he drew a deep breath. She liked it far too much and could dance in his arms the rest of the night. Tony was magic to her, weaving an irresistible spell.

"Let's go to my suite. We can sit and talk if that's what you want." The offer hung in the air. He sounded casual, offhand about the invitation, yet once again she felt this was the moment to say no. She needed to stop the relationship before it ever started, to avoid it altogether. This was an opening to end whatever this was with Tony.

Why was he so irresistible to her? The man wanted to become a billionaire in less than ten years. She wanted to be married and have a family even sooner. They had clashing goals and if she tangled her life with Tony's she would get hurt and delay or even destroy all hope of the family she sought.

She met his dark gaze, knowing he was waiting for an answer while she was torn between yes and no.

Six

"Let's go to my suite. It's just to sit and talk," he repeated.

"That's exactly what I want, Tony. We can do that right here at our table or while we dance."

"I want you all to myself."

"That goes against all good judgment."

"It won't be anything more than you want it to be. C'mon, Isabelle. It isn't a monumental, life-changing decision. One evening. I'll take you to your suite whenever you want. I just want to be with you a while longer."

"Tony, it goes against all good judgment," she said again, sighing. "Why can't I resist you?"

He leaned close. "We can't resist each other. How many other women do you think I've wanted to spend time with when I know their goal in the immediate future is marriage? You're not the only one who knows better yet can't resist."

Surprised, she studied him. She hadn't thought about their relationship from his perspective. Her goal should send him running, but it hadn't. His remark shook her.

"All the more reason—" she began.

"Shh, Isabelle." He looked her in the eyes. "Live dangerously, as the old saying goes. Spend another hour or two with me."

He brushed a light kiss on her lips. "C'mon with me. You can leave whenever you want."

"Tony." She sighed, shaking her head. "You are a spellbinding man." How many times in her life did she get to spend evenings like this one? She told herself she would just stay a short time.

"Good. Just for a while longer together," he said, smiling and taking her hand as they left.

They took the elevator up one floor and stepped out into a short hallway. He unlocked and held open a door. She entered a suite larger and even more luxurious than her own. From a small entryway, they walked into a spacious living area that held one wall of floor to ceiling glass and a staircase to a ground level extension of the room. Through the glass she could see whitecaps. "The view from here in the day must be spectacular."

"I think the view is sensational right now," Tony said in a husky voice, and her cheeks flushed. Desire filled his dark gaze. "I'll build a fire," he said.

She watched as he hunkered down to stack logs in the fireplace and ignite kindling. In minutes he had a roaring fire and she moved toward it. With sundown the temperature had dropped, the air had chilled and now the fire's welcome warmth felt cozy.

A light knock on the door surprised her. She watched while Tony greeted a waiter who wheeled in a cart with a drink and two beers on ice, as well as a bottle of wine on ice. After tipping the waiter, Tony closed the door behind him.

"Before we left the bar I ordered another piña colada for you since you barely touched yours and left it behind in the bar," he said as he brought her drink to her.

"Thank you."

Turning off the lights so they had only the orange glow from the blazing fire, he opened a cold beer for himself and led her to a sofa near the fire. "Sit here and we'll talk." He sat close, turning so he faced her, winding his fingers in her hair while he sipped his beer. "Now tell me about yourself," he said. "Tell me about your family."

For a moment the only sound was the crackle and hiss of the fire. The more details about her life she shared with him, the closer she would be drawn to him and the more deeply she might fall in love with him. His dark eyes were on her and she had his undivided attention. He made everything that involved him too tempting to resist.

"I have two older brothers, a younger brother and a younger sister. In that order they are Josh, Talbot, Trent and Faith. Only Faith is married. There are no grandchildren."

"Any other graphic artists in the family?"

"No. Josh is an accountant in Fort Worth. Talbot has his own construction company in Denton, Trent is a professor at a community college here and Faith is a teacher in Plano. Everyone is in the Dallas area, so we have family get-togethers fairly often." While she talked, he combed his fingers through her hair, so slight, yet still heightening her response.

"My family gets together for some holidays. Sometimes one or another or all of us are scattered because we're traveling," he said.

"What about when you were children?"

"Especially when we were children. We weren't traveling, but our parents often were," Tony replied, caressing her nape, feathery strokes that had a deeper effect and were more sensual. "Do you know a man named Dylan Kinnaly?"

"Yes, I do," she replied, and she hoped he would talk about what he had done for his sister. She had to admire him for that and she wouldn't mind telling him.

"I thought you might through your graphic arts connections. My sister wants to marry him. Dylan is an okay guy and also,

I think my sister knows what she wants. She seems deeply in love."

"He is more than an 'okay guy.' Dylan's a close friend. I think a lot of him."

"That reaffirms my feelings about him. My sister is level-headed. At least she usually is. People in love see the world in a skewed manner."

Isabelle smiled at him. "Don't sound so cynical about people who fall in love."

"Show me someone in love who can think consistently in a clear, rational manner, particularly where the loved one is involved. You won't be able to find anyone. I just see reality."

"No, you don't," she said with a smile. "You're cynical, Tony, when it comes to love."

"Love makes the world go round," he said in a husky voice, and lifted her hair off her shoulders and neck while he leaned close to brush a warm kiss on her nape, stirring a wave of sparks.

"I've met your sister," she said without thought. Her attention was on Tony, his kiss, the faint caresses on her nape, all creating sparks.

"You knew Sydney after you met me or before?"

"I met her afterward. It was a film festival held at one of the local museums. We talked a little because we both are fans of old films. Since then, I've seen her several times with Dylan at graphic arts celebrations or parties. Dylan and I are both members of a Dallas graphic artists' group."

"All this time, Sydney knew you and where to find you? Damn. Why didn't she tell me about you?" His eyes narrowed. "You didn't tell her that you knew me, did you?"

"I didn't see any point in it," she admitted. She would never tell something that might hurt feelings, but she suspected Tony had little experience with rejection from women, and his total self-confidence would keep any hurt feelings from happening.

He studied her with an intense stare. "You really didn't want to see me again?"

"That night was in the past. Since I didn't hear from you, I didn't see any reason to pursue it. You didn't call, come see me—there was no contact. That means you didn't want to see me again. I assumed I would never cross paths with you again. That weekend was magical. Actually, you really charmed me and I had a wonderful time. You brought out a wild side in me that I hadn't shown before or since."

He inhaled deeply. "How I wish I had known all that after our night together. I would never have stopped trying to get back with you. You sound as if you had regrets. I didn't, Isabelle," he stated quietly.

"Not regrets. When you didn't call, I just saw no point in pursuing something that was finished. I've seen occasional pictures of you with society women. You didn't ever call me, so why would I think you'd want to see me?" He slipped his fingers into her hair again. "It no longer matters," she added.

"I just would have found you sooner. How did you get into graphic arts?"

"I've always wanted to pursue graphic arts. I hope to have my own business at some point."

"That may be difficult with all your plans for a family."

"I see my own business as something happening far into the future. At this time in my life, it's just a dream. I've loved my work at Morris."

"I hope you continue to like it. You should, because you have your own department and a lot of authority."

"I'm looking forward to that part of the job and to having my same staff with me."

The corner of his mouth raised in a crooked smile. "So what part are you not looking forward to?"

She smiled in return. "Dealing with my supervisor and trying to keep business and my private life totally separate. So far, I'm failing to do so."

"We're doing pretty well at keeping it separate. Nothing about business has interfered with us tonight."

"You're learning about me. Tell me about you. Other than business, what's in your life in addition to the few things you've mentioned already?"

"When I have time, I play basketball with my friends. I play polo. Travel, swim, play golf. Attend the symphony, the opera. Attend charity balls."

"With your work schedule, I'd say you're spread pretty thin," she remarked, doubting he did half the things he listed on a regular basis. "I think your key words were, 'When I have time.'"

"I make time for the important things. Such as this weekend. This was top priority, definitely," he said, rubbing strands of her hair against his cheek.

"You could have clued me in."

"Would have spoiled the surprise."

"So did all your family get together for this past Christmas holiday?" she asked, wondering what the holidays were like in the Ryder mansion.

"No. My sister went with Dylan to his family's celebration in Waco—not too far. My folks flew to Paris with friends. I went skiing in Switzerland." He glanced at her. "You're looking at me like someone might look at Scrooge."

"Not Scrooge. I guess I just feel sorry for you. I can't imagine a holiday without family."

"You could imagine it if you knew my family. My parents fight when they're home. If they're out doing something, traveling, with friends, then they're okay. Otherwise, they're not the most fun to be around. Plus Dad always has an agenda where Sydney and I are concerned. Until this year. He's backed off trying to manage my life and is now focused on my sister."

"I'm sorry, Tony. I can't conceive of that. Our family times are great fun. I will invite you to go with me to the next big family gathering and you'll see what I'm talking about."

"I look forward to meeting your entire family," he said, but she couldn't believe that he would actually accept such an invitation. She doubted he went home to visit his own family very often. Particularly if his sister wasn't going to be there.

"I'll tell you now—I'm not sure I'd know how to behave in one of those folksy Christmases you see in old movies."

"Then I do feel sorry for you," she said, patting his hand, and he smiled.

"That's a first. I have a lot of firsts with you. You have a few with me."

Her gaze flew to his and they both remembered their night of love when she lost her virginity.

He rubbed his cheek again with locks of her hair. "Temptation," he whispered, his dark gaze on her. "I can't tell you what you do to me. I missed you this week. I'm not even thinking straight. I lose my train of thought at work, something that's never happened before."

Her heart pounded with his confession. She was amazed she had that effect on him. "You're not thinking rationally because of me?" she couldn't resist asking, remembering his description earlier about people in love.

"Don't sound so delighted. No, I'll admit I'm not. Thursday night, I got locked out of my hotel room in the dead of night. After we finished our phone conversation, I stepped out to get more ice and came back to a locked room."

She had to laugh and he grinned. "I got a key from a clerk. You're driving me to distraction, Isabelle."

"I don't believe it, Tony. You're a walking business machine. You're focused on business, living it twenty-four/seven most of the time. You've done a phenomenal job this year, increasing your fortune tremendously."

"Believe me. I'm distracted," he said. "I catch myself lost in thought about you." Each confession placed a tighter hold on her heart. Wisdom told her not to give him credence, yet her heart raced that she was ruffling his ordered, driven lifestyle.

"I don't think as clearly, and locking myself out of my room was a first and totally unlike me," he said, setting his cold beer beside him and turning to her.

"I wish I was having as much influence on you."

She smiled. "I wouldn't tell you if you were," she whispered, more aware of his intent than their conversation. She wanted to close her eyes and raise her mouth for his kiss. She wanted to be in his arms. The culmination of the sexy swimming, dancing and flirting was taking its toll. Just like his effect on her the night they met, his charm, attention and flirting demolished her resolutions and made her behave out of character.

Tony took her drink from her hands and set it on the table.

"Tony..."

He leaned the short distance between them and kissed her, silencing her protest.

Her insides heated while passion overrode all else. She wrapped her arm around his neck and kissed him back. They had been headed for seduction from the moment she had emerged from the depths of the pool and discovered him standing at the far end.

"No seduction, Tony," she whispered as if trying to remind herself to be cautious. Even as she said the words, she showered light kisses on his ear while her hands sought the buttons of his shirt and unfastened them.

"Fair enough," he whispered, peeling away the navy blouse that he had already unbuttoned.

Torn with mixed emotions, losing an inner battle with herself because desire had built to an overwhelming level, she was tossing aside her resolutions. Even though her actions fought her life goals, she had wanted to kiss and caress him since she had watched him plunge into the pool. Now she could yield to impulses that had been storming her senses. As she trailed kisses from his shoulder down to flat male nipples, she ran one hand through chest hair, feeling tight curls against her sensitive palm. Her other hand pushed away his shirt and then caressed his smooth, muscled back. Every touch and kiss, every minute in his arms took her further from her hopes, yet now, tonight, she wanted Tony more than dreams.

She kissed him slowly, tongues intertwined. Always, his kisses were magical, hot, making her want more of him. Mistake upon mistake to say yes, yet she didn't want to resist. Conflicting feelings continued to war. For a few moments she would shut them out and give and take what she wanted. There was still time for no. But for a little while tonight she wanted to live in the present. She could go back to dreams and goals tomorrow.

He slipped off her bra and cupped her breasts while he kissed her. Sensations rocked her. Touching and being touched, again exploring his muscled body. He picked her up easily as he kissed her and set her on his lap, cradling her head against his shoulder, holding her with his arm around her while his caresses heightened passion.

His hand slid beneath her skirt along her bare leg, moving to her inner thigh, light strokes that built the fire already raging. Removing her skirt, he moved her legs apart to pull away her tiny thong and toss it aside. When he caressed her intimately, she arched beneath his touch, gasping with pleasure as she gripped his shoulder. "Tony," she whispered.

Her eyes were squeezed closed while he showered kisses on her breasts, taking her nipple in his mouth. Sensations bombarded her more than ever, driving her to a deeper need.

"Tony," she cried, turning to sit astride and face him. She leaned forward to kiss him while she unbuckled his belt and pulled it away, opening his slacks. Knowing each kiss, caress, move was taking her into deeper involvement, she felt caught in a passionate whirlwind, wanting to never stop, to drive him over a brink of control.

She caressed him until he groaned and held her tightly by her shoulders. Drawing a deep breath, she looked into his brown eyes, to see unmistakable hunger hot and blatant. "A few more minutes, Tony, and then we stop."

"Whatever you want," he whispered while he kissed her between words. His mouth covered hers and he held her tightly against him. Still astride him, she wrapped her arms around his neck.

His hands were everywhere, his mouth taking her kisses. Time and problems didn't exist. Tony overwhelmed all else. Still kissing, he shifted her, placing her on the sofa and coming down on top of her, his thick rod, hot, hard against her.

"I've wanted this," he whispered. "I've dreamed of making love to you," he added, showering kisses, his hand moving between her legs.

His words reminded her of his determination to seduce her, and his hand moving on her intimately was carrying them beyond stopping. Did she want to become Tony's lover? That question cooled her. "Tony," she whispered. "Tony, wait," she said, making an effort to break away, to end the folly. "I can't go on. I'm not ready for this."

He stared at her as if he couldn't fathom what she was telling him. Then he moved away to look at her.

"You're gorgeous. You take my breath. I want to love you again. I remember that night in the smallest detail. I want you, but when we love, I want you to desire it and tell me and show me." All the time he talked, he kissed her lightly and caressed her while she continued to touch him. "The loving was fantastic, Isabelle. I'll wait because that's what I want from you—all your passion."

His words seduced as much as his kisses and caresses. Words

to shake her with wanting him. Words and promises she would never forget and spend hours longing to have happen.

"I can't," she said, moving past him, aware he watched her as she gathered her clothes. He caught up with her, his arm circling her waist, pulling her back against his heated body and thick rod, holding her against him while he stroked her nape with his tongue and his other hand went around her to play with her breasts.

She cried out in pleasure, clinging to his arm, wanting to stop him while hoping he would continue.

"Let me dress. I have to now," she gasped, the words barely audible as her pleasure heightened and her resolve wavered.

"We'll make love, Isabelle. You want to far too badly to keep saying no."

"I want marriage, Tony. You don't. It's that simple. You want to make your billion dollars." She lashed out in the only way she knew would stop both of them.

He stilled and she moved away, gathering her clothes, pulling them on hastily.

He yanked on his clothes swiftly, taking her hand as soon as she was dressed.

She looked up in surprise, thinking he would want her to say good-night.

"Stay and talk. You're good company."

"Always invitations from you that I know I should refuse. Instead, I accept. Talking is almost as dangerous as kissing."

"Not quite," he said, giving her a crooked smile. "Talk is nothing. I talk with Myrtle at great length because she's good company, but that doesn't make it a dangerous pastime."

Isabelle had to laugh. Myrtle Wrightman was the oldest Morris employee, hired by another generation of Morrises. She was an accountant and still sharp and witty and she enjoyed her job.

"That's better," Tony said, smiling at Isabelle. "I like to hear you laugh."

"I'm glad you've found Myrtle and you like her. You do intend to keep her, don't you?"

"Certainly. She's an icon. She does a good job from what I've seen. I wouldn't think of letting her go. Actually, I recommended she get a raise because she hasn't had one in a while."

"I should have qualified my statement and said 'talking to you is almost as dangerous as kissing,'" Isabelle said, sitting in a corner of the sofa, seeing another side of Tony that earned more of her respect for him.

"Want something else? There's a fridge in this suite and it's stocked with drinks and snacks. How about popcorn and cocoa and I'll toss another log on the fire. You don't have to be anywhere in particular in the morning."

"Sounds good, Tony. Let me help."

She followed him to the tiny kitchen and in a short time they sat in front of the fire with popcorn and mugs of steaming hot chocolate while they talked.

As they went from topic to topic without mentioning business, the fire burned to smoldering embers. Finally Isabelle stood. "I have to go. The sun will be coming up in a few hours."

He stood, draping an arm across her shoulders. "I'll see you to your suite—or you can stay here. Either bedroom."

She smiled at him. "I better go to my own suite."

As they headed to her room, he said, "I'll meet you for breakfast unless you want to swim first with me."

"I'll meet you for breakfast," she said, remembering the hot, sexy moments in the pool.

"Great. And after, I'll give you the deluxe tour of San Diego, although I can think of more fun things to show you."

"San Diego is what I really want to see."

At her door, she turned to him. "Thanks, Tony, for a fun evening. I have to admit, I'm glad you flew out here."

"Ah, that makes it all worthwhile," he said. He slid his arm around her waist and kissed her. She put her arms around his waist to return a kiss that soon became *kisses* until she finally stopped.

"It has to be good-night now," she said, breathless, once again on fire with wanting him as if they hadn't spent the past hours together.

"Night, Isabelle," he said in a raspy, husky voice that was seductive. She reminded herself that saying no to Tony was the right decision for her future.

Telling herself to hold to that, she went inside and closed the door, listening to the lock click in place. She had left on lights and in minutes she switched them off and climbed into bed to think about Tony, wanting him, wondering if they were headed for a disaster. Tonight had carried them deeper and closer to an affair. For one brief moment she gave it consideration. Would it interfere so deeply with her goal of marriage? She was still young enough to not have to rush into marriage. She wondered whether she was fooling herself with that argument. Tony was more desirable than any man she had ever known. Would a brief affair be so disastrous?

"Yes, it would," she said aloud. "Get more backbone, Isabelle," she added. For giant reasons, her employer, a man set against marriage, a workaholic, would combine to make an affair a catastrophe. It would be a broken heart for her.

Keeping his promise, Saturday and Sunday Tony showed her the city. He was charming, still flirting, touching her casually: his arm around her shoulders, taking her hand, sitting close beside her, so many light touches that shouldn't have provoked desire, but did. She held to her promise to herself Saturday night and slept alone in her suite.

Sunday night they boarded his plane and flew home with

tension heightening every hour spent together. By the time he saw her to her door, it was midnight Sunday evening.

She unlocked the door and he stepped inside with her while she turned off her alarm.

"I'll always remember this weekend, Tony," she said. "Thank you for a wonderful time."

"I'll remember it, too. Let me take you to dinner tomorrow night." When she opened her mouth to answer, he swooped down to kiss her, drawing her into his embrace and holding her tightly.

All weekend he had charmed her, but she had guarded her heart. Instantly prudence burned away in a blaze of passion that was as passionate as Friday and Saturday nights with him. She dropped her purse and clung to him, kissing him, returning heat for heat, wanting him yet determined to stop.

When she ended their kisses, Tony was as breathless as she was.

"I'll pick you up at seven," he said, and she merely nodded, wanting to reach for him and pull him back.

He turned and was gone, closing the door behind him. She opened it to watch him stride back to the waiting limo and climb inside. She waved, even though she couldn't see him through the limo's tinted glass.

Closing the door, she moved automatically, her thoughts on Tony, wanting him with her. She was falling in love with him.

She acknowledged what she felt in her heart. Loving Tony would be hopeless. An affair with him would be meaningless and disturbing because she never wanted a relationship without commitment and had avoided one all these years. Until now. Unless she moved on and got away from Tony, that's exactly what she was going to get herself involved in. She couldn't exist in a relationship without a commitment. Her heart would be in it totally. And get broken to pieces in the process.

"Move on and save yourself grief," she whispered. She suspected sleep would be a long time in coming.

Since Isabelle would be present, Tony looked forward to the Monday-morning staff meeting with an eagerness he had never had before. All his presidents and vice presidents attended and they went over any significant items for the upcoming week or month.

He was talking to Porter Haswell when others began to file into the room and the moment Isabelle stepped through the doorway, the air became electric. He continued listening to Porter, but flicked a glance at Isabelle, taking in her wine-colored suit with a matching blouse. With her hair pinned up again, she was buttoned up, looking business as usual, except the skirt ended at her knees, revealing shapely calves and trim ankles.

Tonight she would have dinner with him. He suspected she had been about to refuse his dinner invitation when he had kissed away a reply. Sometimes a twinge of guilt plagued him for his efforts to win her over and take her away from her goal of marriage and a family. If someone treated his sister in such a manner, he would be furious. Yet, Isabelle was so damned responsive to him, plus beautiful, sexy and appealing in every possible way. She had made it evident that she desired him and that she had found their night of love together something unique and special in her life. How could he walk away from all that?

He tried to focus on Porter when he felt his phone vibrate. Tony glanced at his phone and saw a text from his sister asking him if he could meet her for a quick lunch. It had their own code for "highly important" with an exclamation point accompanying the message.

He stepped into the hall to send her a quick reply telling her he would meet her and naming a restaurant. Wondering what had happened to cause her request, he returned to the meeting.

He met Isabelle's wide blue eyes and again, the air sparked. He deliberately looked elsewhere, feeling the tension between them. Ruffling through papers on the table, he focused on the meeting, trying to keep his mind off the prospect of dinner with her tonight. When he looked at her or was with her, any slight guilt he felt for wanting to pursue her faded away.

The minute the meeting concluded, she gathered her things and headed out without a glance at Tony.

Thirty minutes before noon Tony left the office for the downtown Dallas club where he and his family, as well as most of his close friends, had memberships.

As he emerged from the elevator on the top floor and walked toward the club restaurant, he heard a familiar greeting.

"Hey, Tony."

Tony looked around to see Gabe Benton in Western boots, jeans and a jacket over a white shirt that was open at the throat. "Going to lunch?" Gabe asked. "I just finished."

"I'm meeting Sydney for lunch. You look in a rush."

"I have a cattle auction to attend."

Tony smiled. "I'm amazed your dad has left you alone about pursuing a ranching career instead of oil. You're a good petroleum engineer, and Jake relies on you a lot. Actually, you're a good investment broker."

Gabe grinned. "What my dad doesn't know won't hurt him. He doesn't hear much about ranching from either Jake or me. I love it, Tony. I'm a cowboy at heart. Too much time with Grandpa Wade when I was growing up."

"Looks like damned hard work for uncertain returns if you ask me," Tony said.

"As if any of the rest of you have certain returns on the deals you make."

Tony smiled. "Go buy a lot of cows."

"Cattle. Tell Sydney hi. Tell her to hang in there if she's still getting flack from your dad."

"I'm sure she's still getting that. I'll tell her," Tony said. "Take it easy." He entered the restaurant as Gabe went striding away.

Tony's thoughts shifted fully to Sydney. Something bad had happened. He could tell from her terse text message. He wondered what his father had done now. Or had Dylan given her a final goodbye and severed all ties? He knew there was no point in worrying or guessing. In minutes, he would know, because he would hear as soon as she arrived.

He was a few minutes early as he had planned. He wanted a table ready when Sydney appeared. He didn't want her to have to wait for him.

He tipped the maître d', whom he knew well, to seat him in a quiet place away from others. The table, in a corner beside a window overlooking downtown, was perfect. He was on the twenty-seventh floor and the view was spectacular, but Tony barely glanced at it as he saw his sister following the maître d' toward him.

With her black curls in a tangle and her clothing rumpled, Sydney looked as if a catastrophe had befallen her. A few feet from the table he saw her tears shimmer and he wondered what new threat his father had given Sydney. He couldn't think of anything else to bring her to the disheveled state she was in. He braced to hear the worst.

Seven

Sydney's sad expression made his insides tighten. Evidently, her news was worse than he had expected. "Dammit," he whispered under his breath, clenching his fists and trying to curb his anger. Not to mention reminding himself again that his father must never interfere with his own life again.

"Hi, Sydney," Tony said, holding her chair, his gaze racing over her. It was a mild shock to see her. In the past days, she had lost weight. Her curls were tangled and she was pale. His worry deepened, and he braced for some really grim news.

"Thanks, Tony, for meeting me when you had such short notice." He sat across from her, waiting in silence for her to tell him her troubles in her own time. The waiter appeared to take their drink orders, returning in minutes with water and a small pot of hot tea for Sydney.

As soon as the waiter took their orders for salads and left them alone Sydney rummaged in her purse. She withdrew a folded envelope and gave it to him. "Here's your money back, Tony. I appreciate that money more than you'll ever know."

"What's bringing this on?"

Her eyes filled with tears and she looked away. He waited in silence, certain she would answer his question when she regained her composure. Finally she faced him as she wiped her eyes.

"I'm sorry. I really loved Dylan. I guess I made a poor choice. I was wrong about him. I'm giving you back your money because everything is rosy between Mom, Dad and me now. I won't be disinherited and Dad will pay for medical school. Dylan is gone for good."

"What happened with Dylan?" Tony asked, feeling a rising tide of anger if Dylan had hurt Sydney, yet still puzzled how he could have hurt her this badly.

She looked away again. The waiter came with salads for both of them and they sat in silence while they were served. As soon as the waiter left, Sydney pushed her plate aside and leaned closer over the table.

"Dylan broke off with me because Dad paid him a lot of money to do so."

Tony clenched his fist, which was in his lap and out of Sydney's sight. Fury suffused him, making him hot. "Damn, Sydney, I'm sorry," he said, as angry with his father as he was with Dylan. "Sydney, if Dylan is that kind of man, you're better off to find it out now."

"Common sense tells me that. I loved him. I thought he loved me," she said, looking away and biting her lip.

"That happens, Syd. It's hard to really know someone else. When did this happen?"

"Last Friday. Dad called me and told me he wanted to see me. When I went by the house, he told me that he would continue to support me in med school and he was not changing his will since Dylan was out of my life."

"We talked a little and then he told me just what you said now, that it was better to find out about Dylan now than later. I told him that Dylan left me because he didn't want me hurt. Dad just smiled as if dealing with a five-year-old. When he did that, I knew something was wrong."

"Dammit, I'm so sorry," Tony repeated, knowing full well the look Sydney had received. His father was always smug when he had the upper hand and had manipulated matters to get what he wanted.

"He told me that wasn't why Dylan left. That it was in his best interests to do so. That's when he told me he paid Dylan twenty-five thousand dollars to get out of my life and stay out." She looked stricken as she gazed at Tony, and his sympathy for her deepened.

"By Dad's standards, it wasn't much money. That's the irony of it. Dad would have paid a lot more." She turned away and put her handkerchief on her eyes, crying silently. "I'm sorry I'm getting so emotional. I've been able to hold it together with Mom and Dad, but I can't with you."

"Don't worry about tears. Dammit, Sydney, where does Dylan work?"

Her head jerked around. "Don't go talking to Dylan. Or worse, don't go punching him."

"I'm not going to hit him," Tony stated, although he didn't add that he would like to. "What did Dylan say when you confronted him about it?"

"I haven't. I don't want to ever see him again. We haven't been seeing each other, anyway. He's cut all ties and won't take my calls. Now I know why. A deal he made with Dad," she added bitterly. "I can't even feel angry with Dad. It's Dylan who tears me up with what he did."

Tony wanted to leave the restaurant and find Dylan and tell him what he thought of him. He knew it was a knee-jerk reaction, but he was furious that his sister had been so badly treated. "I have to agree, Sydney. I can't get as angry with Dad as I do with Dylan for being insincere and cheap. You're so much better off without him. The man you fell in love with obviously wasn't the real Dylan. He pulled the wool over my eyes, too, Syd. I thought he was really a great guy. He seemed as sincere as possible and I'm accustomed to dealing with men trying to fool me."

"I know," she said in a hollow voice. She gripped Tony's hand. "Promise me you won't go see Dylan."

"I'm not doing any such thing. I promise I won't hit him," Tony said, hoping he could keep that promise, because right now he would like to punch Dylan. "Where does he work, Sydney? I won't hurt him. I can find out from someone else if you won't tell me."

"It's over, Tony. Just let it go. I want to give you this check."

"You ought to just keep it, Syd. Now, where does Dylan work?"

She bit her lip and sighed. "He works for L.J. Luxury Yachts. He's head of their advertising department. Tony, don't worry me about Dylan."

"I won't hurt him and I'm not going to worry you. I think you should have talked to him."

"I didn't see any point in it and I…" Her voice trailed away. "I don't know if I can control my emotions. It's difficult enough with you. I don't want to get all weepy around Dylan. Tony, it hurts and it's scary to think how I misjudged him."

"Sorry, Syd. I'm going to dinner tonight with Isabelle. I'm sure she would be happy if you joined us. You two know each other."

"Through Dylan." As she wiped her eyes, she smiled at him. "You're the best brother possible. Thanks, but I'll be busy until late and then too tired for words. That's one thing—I'm too occupied to dwell on this all day."

"If you're going to work late, you ought to try to eat something."

"I don't see you eating," she said, smiling at him.

They looked at each other and smiled. She took a bite and

sipped her hot tea while Tony also ate a little. His appetite was gone, but he knew it would be a long afternoon for him and he hoped if he ate, Sydney would.

"Take the check, Tony," she said, pushing it closer to him.

He pocketed it without looking at it while Sydney took one more bite and then put aside her fork.

"There's one more thing I want you to do for me. I'd really rather you didn't even talk to Dylan. Promise me you won't retaliate or do anything to him, either."

"Sydney, when have I ever done anything like that?" he asked, even though that's what he longed to do. "There's a law against assaulting someone. I don't want to complicate my life with a crime, so stop worrying."

"I'll take that as a promise," she said. "I'm going to have to get back." She leaned closer to him. "And no, I'm not giving you Dylan's phone number or address. I know you can get someone to give it to you, but please, don't bother. Tony, don't even talk to him about this. Don't make me worry and stop confiding in you."

"If that's what you want, I promise I won't talk to him."

"I'm relieved. Thanks for seeing me on such short notice and for brotherly sympathy. Thanks for everything."

"I'm sorry, Syd," he said, standing when she did. She smiled at him, picked up her purse and left.

As Tony headed back to his office, his thoughts were on Dylan.

He entered the elevator, surprised Isabelle was there along with five other employees. In spite of his simmering anger over Dylan, his heartbeat increased at the sight of her. Memories of the weekend were vivid, taunting him. He wanted to take her into his arms right now. Instead, he returned greetings, some reserved, some with smiles and friendly tones. By the time they were three floors away from Isabelle's office, they were the only two people remaining in the elevator.

"Tony, when I saw you before lunch you said you were going to see your sister. Is everything all right?"

"No. Dylan turned out not to be the man she thought he was. Or you think he is, for that matter. I've promised her I won't even talk to him, but I'm not happy about it."

"Dylan?" Isabelle frowned. "Dylan is as straight an arrow as they come. He's up-front, sincere, friendly. I don't know what happened between them. I didn't think they were even still seeing each other."

"They're not, but not for the noble reasons you attributed to him."

"What are you talking about? Dylan decided to stop seeing her so she wouldn't lose touch with her family, or be disinherited or lose your father's support for med school."

"My father paid Dylan to stop seeing her," Tony snapped. "Dylan accepted the money." They reached her floor and he held the close door elevator button. "I don't know which I'm more annoyed with, Dylan or my father."

Isabelle stared at him with a slight frown. She shook her head. "That doesn't sound like Dylan."

"Women are so damn softhearted. It makes them gullible."

Isabelle's frown grew more fierce. "Is that so? I've known Dylan a long time. That doesn't sound like him. Frankly, if he had accepted money to stop seeing your sister, knowing Dylan as I do, I think he would have told me."

"You're that close with him?" Tony ground out the words, beginning to wonder what kind of relationship she had with Dylan.

"No, we're not that close. Dylan is that *forthright* about what he does," Isabelle lashed out, making him realize that in his anger, he had jumped to baseless conclusions about how close she had been to Dylan. He surprised himself because his reaction smacked of jealousy, something he had never felt before in his life. "Has Sydney talked to Dylan about taking money from your dad?"

Tony studied her, lost in thought about what she was telling him, as well as his reaction, and barely hearing her question. "You really think that doesn't sound like Dylan?" he asked, an idea occurring to him that he didn't want to face.

"Yes," she said flatly. "I'm due in an appointment."

"Be a minute late. I need to pursue this a moment. Isabelle, I promised Sydney I wouldn't talk to Dylan. Will you speak to him for me? If Dylan didn't get paid by Dad to leave Sydney, my father made that up."

"Surely not," Isabelle said, staring at Tony as if he had grown another head. "How could he meddle in her life with a lie that she's bound to discover some day? When she caught him, she would be furious or hate him."

"She might discover it and she might not. Sydney and Dylan have stopped all contact. If she's hurt and angry and Dylan has moved on, she'll never know. If Dad—I can't even say it—if he lied about the money, there's a chance Dylan wouldn't ever hear about it. My dad may have been willing to take the risk. The odds are, no one would find out."

"No father would do that," Isabelle whispered, still staring at Tony.

"I didn't think mine would ever stoop that low—he never has, but he's angry about losing control over me. He's furious with Sydney." Tony grasped her shoulder. "Isabelle, I promised Sydney I wouldn't talk to Dylan. Will you ask Dylan for me? Tell him what's happened. I can count on you for the truth."

"You don't even know me that well," she said.

"Yes, I do. Will you do that for me? Hell, do it for Sydney and Dylan. If you and Sydney are right about him, he's getting blamed for something he knows nothing about."

"That's appalling."

"Stop looking at me as if I'm the one who did it. I'm not like my father."

"You're driven and so is he."

"I'm driven to succeed to get him off my back. You can't imagine how manipulative he is." He paused as what he just said made him stop and think. "I never caught him in a lie, but he has gone to great lengths to manipulate things to get his way. I'm not like him, Isabelle, I swear. I would never do something dishonest like this. I didn't think he would. If it weren't for you…no one would know the truth here," he said. "Isabelle and I wouldn't know that Dylan didn't accept the money."

"Tony, I've got to get to my meeting," she said, glancing at her watch. "This truly doesn't sound like Dylan, so I'll talk to him for you and for all three of you. If Dylan hasn't taken money from your father, it would terrible for Sydney and Dylan if they never learned the truth."

"Thanks, Isabelle," Tony said, releasing the button so the doors would open. He watched her walk away, her hips swaying slightly, her skirt ending above her knees, giving him a look at her long shapely legs. She halted and glanced back. "I'll let you know. I'll try to talk to him as soon as possible."

He nodded, still watching her, lost in his thoughts. Anger and shock tormented him. How could his father lie to get his way? Yet Tony could imagine, when his dad lost his power over his son and at the same time had his daughter go against his wishes, taking a last, desperate measure to remain in control. And how was Tony to know what his dad had done in the past?

All afternoon, it was an effort to keep his mind on business instead of his father, Sydney, Dylan—and Isabelle. Once in a meeting, he caught a vice president and close friend staring at him, making him wonder what he had just said in answer to a question he also didn't recall. He tried to focus on the meeting, but in minutes his thoughts drifted back to Isabelle again.

At five he received a text from Isabelle, stating that she would like to see him. He sent a message in return to come to his office.

Within minutes, he heard a knock and looked up to see her waiting in the doorway.

"Come in," he said, standing to walk around his desk.

"Your secretary has gone. Her computer is off," Isabelle said, closing the door behind her.

"She leaves at five o'clock. Damn, I'm glad to see you," he said when Isabelle crossed the room. He met her, taking her into his arms to kiss her.

"Tony—"

His kiss ended whatever she had been about to say. She resisted only seconds and then wrapped her arms around him to kiss him back, setting him ablaze. He wanted to peel off the business clothes and take down her hair, but this wasn't the time or place. She would never let him do that in his office, anyway.

His pulse thundered, shutting out other sounds. He was aroused and tightened his arm around her, wanting to kiss her and not stop. He shifted slightly as he held her with one arm. His other hand slid lower, caressing her throat, easing down to the full curve of her soft breast.

"Tony, this is your office. I don't want to walk out of here looking as if we've been making love."

"We're probably alone on this floor."

"I need to talk to you," she said, walking away and straightening her clothes, winding a few locks of her hair back in place. "I'm going to dinner tonight with Dylan. I'll have to reschedule our dinner."

"Oh, hell," he said, disappointed, torn between wanting to tell her to cancel with Dylan and thanking her for agreeing to question Dylan about the money as soon as possible. "I hate that, but if it helps Sydney, I'll agree. Tomorrow night, then, unless there's hope of seeing you after you leave Dylan."

She smiled at him. "I won't be late with Dylan, but I will have already eaten and it's a work night, so I should just go home then."

"I want to hear from you as soon as you know the truth about the money. I don't want to wait until tomorrow. Sydney looked awful today. She isn't eating, probably not sleeping and studying like crazy. Send me a text or call me when you leave the restaurant. I'll meet you."

"I'll do that. The sooner you hear the truth, the better. I don't know your father, but I do know Dylan. I feel certain about him."

"Either way, I'm going to be unhappy about it. Dad has never done anything like this before. At least not that I know about. If he hasn't paid Dylan, it will make me wonder if he's ever lied about something in the past to get his way. Hell of a deal either way."

"I need to finish a letter before I leave to meet Dylan. I have to go."

He nodded. "I've been looking forward all day to dinner tonight," he said, walking to the elevator with her, catching her for a brief kiss that he wanted to lengthen, but she stepped away. "I'll be waiting for your call after you leave Dylan."

She nodded. "It'll probably be about nine or nine-thirty when Dylan and I part."

When the elevator doors closed behind her, Tony returned to his desk. In minutes he could focus on business because Isabelle had taken over and would help with his family problem. For just an instant, he thought about how important she was becoming to him and in his life.

It was a new experience and not one he wanted to explore, so he forced himself to concentrate on his work.

At six Isabelle entered the restaurant. It was startling to see Dylan, because he had lost weight and had a somber expression she had never seen before. Unlike his usually cheerful optimistic self, he stood and held her chair, barely speaking, appearing intensely unhappy.

"You miss her, don't you?" Isabelle asked when he sat facing her.

He looked away and a muscle worked in his jaw. "I thought I would begin to get over this. Instead, it gets a little worse each day that passes. I've never been in love before, Isabelle, never like this. Sydney has stopped calling, stopped trying to get me to change my mind. I suppose she's getting over it."

He paused as a waitress appeared and they placed orders for water, plus hot tea for Isabelle. "How's it going with you and the brother?"

She wanted to keep the conversation about Sydney going, but didn't want to rush into questions. "He surprised me by flying to San Diego last weekend when I was there for business."

He attempted a smile. "Did you have a good time?"

"Yes. That's never been the problem. But unlike Sydney, who wants to marry, Tony wants to avoid marriage or commitment."

"I doubt if he'll change," Dylan said. "He's in his thirties and has avoided serious entanglements so far."

"His work is his main interest." She paused while their waitress brought water and took their orders. "Dylan, I want to ask something that's very personal and if you don't want to answer my question, I'll understand."

"Ask away. We're close friends. I can't imagine any question you have that I will mind answering."

She sipped her water, wondering if Dylan would still feel that way after she asked him such a personal question. "Did Sydney's father offer you money to stop seeing her?"

"Yes, he did," Dylan said, and Isabelle got a knot in her throat. Shocked that she had misjudged Dylan, too, she stared at him.

"So you stopped seeing her and now you wish you hadn't?"

"Hell, no. He just offered me money this week. I wasn't too

polite about turning him down." His eyes narrowed and he studied her.

"Oh, Dylan!" she exclaimed, swamped with relief. "You told him no, that you wouldn't take his money."

"Damn right. I wasn't nice about it. You thought that was why I stopped seeing her? What's going on, Isabelle? How'd you hear about the money offer?"

"Tony said that Sydney's father told her he paid you to stop seeing her, that his money was why you wouldn't see her again."

"Hell's bells," Dylan snapped, his eyes flashing with fire as his face flushed. "She believed that?"

"Tony told me that she did. At first Tony was shocked when I said I didn't believe it, that you're always so straightforward about everything, and that I was sure you would have told me if you had done that. I think you would have told Sydney."

"She believed him."

"Dylan, stop and think. Both Sydney and Tony were shocked when they heard about it. Tony said his dad had never done anything that dishonest before. I haven't spoken to Sydney, but Tony believed me when I said I didn't think you had."

"So that's why the urgent dinner tonight."

"Yes. Now don't be angry with Sydney."

He blinked and sat in silence. Their dinners were placed on the table, a chicken salad for Isabel, a hamburger for Dylan. She began to eat, trying to give Dylan a chance to think about what she had told him.

"I feel so relieved that you are the person I think you are and Sydney will be, too," Isabelle said finally. "Tony said she has been heartbroken lately and he's worried about her. I'm going to see him when I leave you. He'll call Sydney to tell her."

"I'll tell her myself. That does it. I'm going to see her tonight if I have to knock down her door."

Isabelle smiled. "I'm sure she'll see you. She doesn't know

I'm with you. That was Tony's plan to find out the truth. He promised Sydney he wouldn't talk to you."

"She was probably afraid of what he'd do. I know how I would have felt if it had been my sister." He set down his glass of water. "Isabelle, do you mind finishing dinner on your own? I'll buy your dinner and you can take your time to eat. I'm not hungry at all now. I'm going to see Sydney."

"You don't want me to break the news first?"

"No."

"Dylan, someone has already warned me to beware of Tony because of his family. Sydney is a Ryder, too."

"She'd never do anything dishonest like her father telling her I accepted the money he offered to stop seeing her when that wasn't true. She's ethical and truthful. She's not as driven as the men in the family."

"I'm sure that's true."

"Thanks. Thanks for having so much faith in me and for telling me. I never would have known otherwise."

"Go, Dylan. See if you can find her."

"I'll find her," he said, and left bills on the table to more than cover both dinners. He was gone before she could protest. She watched him hurry across the restaurant and disappear outside.

She called Tony and made arrangements to meet him right away. Her appetite had vanished, too, and she didn't care to linger and eat alone.

When she entered the lot and parked where they agreed to meet, Tony drove up behind her car, reached across to hold open the door. "Get in," he said.

As soon as she had closed the car door, he drove off. "Where are we going?" she asked. "I thought we were going to have a drink here and talk. Mainly talk. I don't need a drink unless it's tea."

"I know a better, quieter place. I've missed being with you. Tell me about Dylan."

"Dylan was shocked. He has not taken a dime from your dad."

"Oh, damn. I'm glad for Sydney's sake." Tony inhaled deeply, unclenching his fists on the steering wheel. After a few moments of silence, he said, "I feel like a kid again, disappointed to discover my parent isn't perfect and the giant I thought he was."

"You dad is human, a man accustomed to getting his way. You, Sydney and Dylan have thwarted him and he lashed out. I'm not defending him, because I think such meddling is despicable," Isabelle answered, turning slightly in the seat to look at Tony.

"You're still lumping us in together. I can hear it in your voice."

"Tony, you're accustomed to getting your way. Have a reputation as a ruthless businessman," she said, not mentioning that he had tried everything to manipulate her into an affair with him. "You're his son. The acorn never falls far from the tree sort of thing."

"Dammit, Isabelle, I haven't ever crossed the line like that to meddle in personal lives or to lie to get what I want. I've bluffed in poker and in business deals, I'll admit, but that's different than what my father did to his child. I've never done anything dishonest like that." He glanced at her while they waited at a red light in a busy intersection. When she didn't reply, he shook his head. "You don't believe me, do you?"

He had to return his attention to the road as the light changed to green.

"It depends on how far you went with it. Poker—that's part of the game and that's nothing. In business, that could mean anything from a harmless exaggeration to something that was totally misleading."

"Ask around. I may have a reputation as ruthless, but I think I also have one as being honest. Where I get the ruthless reputation is for what I'm doing at Morris, trying to streamline and update an old company. That doesn't always sit well with those who have worked there a long time."

"Tony, the main thing here is that Dylan knew nothing about this. He's gone to see Sydney now."

"He won't find her except by cell phone. I told her to wait at my house, that I was bringing you with me and we both wanted to see her."

"That was a little premature, wasn't it?" she asked, surprised Tony trusted her judgment of Dylan that much.

"I think you know your friend. What's more important here than talking to Sydney is that I don't lose your respect. Sydney can learn the truth from Dylan."

She was more touched than she wanted to be. "You haven't lost my respect," she said softly.

"You mean that, don't you?"

Their eyes met for a moment. "I mean it."

He took a deep breath and was silent.

She watched as tall wrought-iron gates opened for them. "So I'll see where you live."

"Yes, you will. I'll take you home when you want. Sydney will fly out of here to see Dylan when she finds out he wants to talk to her. I haven't told her why, just to come out, that I wanted to talk to her."

"I'll be happy to see her again—if I do. I'm sure Dylan has talked to her by now. You do recall this is a work night?"

"Yes. We won't stay late if you don't want to. I've missed you, Isabelle, and looked forward to being with you tonight— all evening with you—but then our plans had to change."

"I'm glad the truth came out." She turned to look at the grounds. Even though it was night, there were lights in the trees and along the driveway, so anyone could see some of the landscaping in the semidarkness. The grounds were tree filled, bare branches in the winter, but she could imagine how beautiful it would be in the other three seasons.

"Tony, this is pretty." They swept around the driveway to pull up in front and Isabelle gazed around when she stepped out of the car. "What a beautiful home you have. I'm surprised. I wouldn't have guessed you'd like one of these older homes. This isn't where you grew up, is it?" she asked, looking at a sprawling three-story stone and wood house with an immense portico to the east. Tall bronze torches flickered at the foot of the steps to the front porch.

"No, not here. I lived in a house like it. It's comfortable, secluded, has good security and it's close enough to downtown Dallas for a short commute." He took her arm to cross a wide porch that held two stately bronze dogs flanking the enormous door with beveled glass panes. Tall china pots with towering banana plants were beside each dog and pots of blooming flowers dotted the porch that held a swing, plus elegant wooden furniture.

The front door opened and Sydney Ryder stood facing them with a slight frown as she glanced from one to the other.

"What's going on, Tony? Dylan has called me several times on my cell phone and tried to talk. I refused to talk to him. I don't know what he wanted. Now here you are, wanting to talk. I'm not sure I want to hear one more disastrous announcement. What's happened, Tony?"

Eight

"Why don't you let us come in and talk," Tony said.

Sydney's eyes widened and she stepped back, motioning to them. "Sorry. Come in, please."

Isabelle smiled, hoping she hid her shock at the sight of Sydney, who was far thinner than she remembered and with dark circles under her eyes. Sydney's hair was an unkempt tangle, and her plain jeans and T-shirt looked as if she had been sleeping in them, and were far too inadequate for the chill in the night air. She held a sweater in her hand that she pulled on.

"Isabelle, it's been a long time since I last saw you," Sydney said.

"It's nice to see you, and part of my reason for being here is good news." Isabelle looked up at Tony, placing her hand on his arm. "Why don't we let Sydney go so she can call Dylan back."

Sydney stared at them. "Why would I—" She glanced between her brother and Isabelle, her expression softening. "Now I am puzzled. What?"

Tony nodded. "Isabelle's right. Go call Dylan and we can talk later."

"I assume as soon as I talk to Dylan, I'll understand all this mystery. Now I'm too curious. I'm going to call him. Sorry to say hello and goodbye in the same breath."

"That's all right, Syd," Tony replied. "We'll see you another time."

Sydney looked at both of them. "If you're in on this, my brother, the news must involve Dad's money. I'm gone. Thanks, maybe, to both of you." She turned to rush down the hall.

Isabelle smiled when she looked at Tony. "I think they're really in love. I've never seen Dylan the way he looked tonight. Or your sister for that matter."

"That's for damn sure. I've never seen Sydney such a wreck. Hopefully, this will work out and they'll be happy again. Now stop worrying about Dylan and Sydney. The staff doesn't live here and they are all away tonight, so we have the house to ourselves. Come here," he said, pulling Isabelle to him while his tone changed, dropping to a velvety note that warmed her.

Switching off the entryway lights, he wrapped her into his embrace. "I missed you terribly."

"We were together yester—"

His kiss ended their conversation. She wrapped her arms around him, her heart racing while she thought *foolish, foolish.* Tony's kisses were addictive, drawing her closer to a relationship.

"You're beautiful," he whispered, brushing feathery kisses on her temple, down to her ear, lower to her throat. "You take my breath away when I look at you and remember loving you."

Every word made her heart pound while she tried to hang on to her resolve. "I thought we weren't going to do this. I came to talk to Sydney and that reason is gone now. Tony, you're being manipulative. I suppose it's in your genes." How would she ever resist him? Her heart raced because she wanted to put her arms around him while she kissed him.

"I'm trying to ignore that one," he whispered. "You can't imagine how I want you."

When he brushed kisses on her temple, she closed her eyes, standing immobile, torn by conflicting feelings. "Have you even heard what I've been saying to you?"

"I've heard you," he answered, his fingers caressing her nape as lightly as his kisses, equally devastating. Did she really want to keep fighting him when she was already in love with him? How tempting to let go and accept a relationship, to see where it would take them and to have Tony's friendship.

He continued trailing kisses to her ear. "Let go of your worries about tomorrow, Isabelle. For this night live in the present and take what you want," he said, echoing her thoughts. His breath was warm on her ear, producing its own erotic effect. "You've got all your tomorrows to say no."

Mesmerizing words. Suggestions her heart wanted more with each passing minute.

His light kisses became kindling for a raging fire, his words even more seductive. She slid her arm around his neck and turned her head slightly as he brushed kisses on her cheek. When her mouth met his, her insides clenched.

His arm tightened around her waist as his mouth opened hers and his tongue won the battle.

She wanted all of him, wanted him inside her. Would he fall in love? She knew better. His heart was already committed to work. Even if he fell in love, work would come first before a family. She never wanted to become deeply involved with a man whose business goal would consume him and now she teetered on the brink of doing just that.

In spite of his manipulative manner, he had become important to her and she could not keep from loving him for his caring for Morris employees, his love and loyalty to his sister, and his generosity with her—all admirable, even if he had an ulterior motive in giving her such a big promotion. His good qualities impressed her. On top of attraction, they were too potent and beguiling.

Letting go, she kissed him in return. His tongue went deep, stirring sensations. She responded with surging passion. This was what she wanted, knowing it as surely now as she had that long-ago night when she'd first met him. The dangers, the outcome, the consequences, all the threats to her peace of mind dwindled away. Barriers and warnings crumbled. She paused to open her eyes to look at him. "Tonight...Tony."

His brown eyes blazed with desire. His arm tightened, recaptured her and he returned to kissing her possessively, demanding a response, eliciting passion so easily.

Her heart thudded as she reacted, winding her fingers in his hair, pouring out all her pent-up longing while desire consumed her. This night would ultimately prove her undoing and break her heart. Even so, she wanted this time together. She would never forget it. She had no idea how long it would take to recover from it. She intended to make certain he never forgot this night with her. There was a depth to Tony and he did care about the people important to him. She intended to become one of them. From what he'd said, she might already be to some degree.

She wound her fingers in his hair while her other hand went to the buttons on his shirt. She unfastened the few at the top and as they kissed, she tugged the shirt from his slacks to shove it off.

While they continued to kiss, she ran her hands across his broad shoulders, remembering and rediscovering, wanting to know every inch, to kiss and caress until he was wild with passion.

While he kissed her, he picked her up in his arms. Kissing him in return, she was unaware where he carried her until he set her on her feet beside a bed.

He shifted her to unfasten her blouse, letting it fall around her feet, followed by her skirt. Slithers of silk and cotton under-garments, fragile barriers removed and tossed aside.

Resting his hands on her waist, Tony languidly looked at her from her chin to her toes and back, meeting her gaze. "I've dreamed of this," he whispered. "Wanting you, thinking how I would like to make love to you, slowly, inch by inch, to pleasure you to the utmost."

"Tony," she whispered, his seductive words working their effect. Clinging to him, she pulled his head close to kiss him ardently. Having made her decision, she let go all caution. She wanted him with a desperate urgency.

Her hands tangled in his thick chest curls and then lowered to unfasten his belt. She freed him from his clothes. She rubbed against him. Warm, bare bodies, soft against hard, light contacts that fueled blazing desire.

He cupped her breasts in his hands, stroking her nipples with his thumbs before he bent to take a taut bud in his mouth. His tongue drew moist circles, each stroke driving her need for fulfillment.

Rocking back, she gasped with pleasure, her eyes closed tightly while she clutched his forearms. Sensations bombarded her, the world spinning into nonexistence except for Tony.

His fingers ran along her hip, his hand slipping between her legs, finding her intimate places. Hidden, private places opening to him. When she gasped and arched against his hand, his mouth came down hard on hers.

She held him with one arm around his neck, her other hand still roaming over his chest and stomach.

His caresses made her moan, the sound muffled by their kisses. Pleasure rocked her. Lifting her again, he placed her on the bed. He knelt beside her, watching her as he picked up her foot to brush light kisses on her ankle.

"Turn over," he said, rolling her slightly until she was on her stomach. His kisses continued along her calf. She dug her nails into the bed, while desire to have more of him increased with each kiss he lavished on her.

Moving with thorough deliberation, he continued trailing kisses up the back of her thighs, his lips warm, so light. The intertwined torment and pleasure overwhelmed. Moaning, she started to roll over, but Tony's hand put slight pressure on the small of her back.

"Wait," he whispered, his kisses lingering on her inner thighs. She tried to spread her legs but was hampered by Tony's legs as he straddled her. "Tony," she gasped, his name merely a hoarse whisper. Need and pleasure racked her. She continued to clutch the bed as sensations showered her.

His tongue was hot, wet along her inner thigh, moving higher, his warm breath another tease, all building desire

"Tony," she gasped, rolling over to look at him as he was on his knees, his thick rod, hard and ready. Beads of sweat gave a sheen to his skin while his bulging muscles were highlighted.

She took his thick rod in her hand, trailing her tongue on him, wanting to stir his passion as much as he had hers.

Closing his eyes and inhaling deeply, he wound his hands in her hair as his breathing grew ragged. He groaned while she continued and then took him in her mouth, her tongue driving him to the brink.

He pulled her up and she looked into his dark eyes. In that moment she felt desired in a manner she never had before—not even that first night when they had both been lighthearted and carefree, just having fun. She had felt desired then, but there was a breathtaking, earnest quality tonight that had not been part of their first night. He wanted her, and the devastating depth of need in his expression all by itself became its own seduction, making her shake and reach for him to kiss him.

Leaning over to kiss her passionately, he wrapped her in his embrace. It was a kiss like none other, passionate, possessive, demanding, consuming her. His kiss fanned her desire into a raging need for all of him, to go beyond caresses and kisses. Her body responded, every inch tingling, aching for him. It was a kiss to never be forgotten, binding her to him this night in an event that would be locked in memory.

It was a kiss that sealed her response to him with no turning back. Her thundering pulse drove out all sounds while she could feel his pounding heart against her own.

She held his strong body, wanting the kiss to never end, at the same time wanting more now. She wanted beyond kisses, wanted Tony with all her being. His arousal was hard against her. He was ready.

She pushed him down to lavish kisses over him, moving to his legs as he had done. Her tongue moved across the back of his knee, up over his inner thigh while he groaned and knotted his fists. Her hands caressed him while she showered light kisses on him. Aware she was in love with him, she ceased to think beyond that point.

His body was strong, hard and masculine, setting her ablaze. Desire intensified while she wanted to prolong their loving, making it last far into the night. She took her time, slowing and doing all she could to pleasure him before he rolled over and she was astride him, gazing into brown eyes that had darkened to midnight while smoldering with desire.

She smiled at him as she caressed his chest and then moved down. Her hair spilled over both of them when she leaned down to trail her tongue over him, more kisses and touches that she hoped pleasured and consumed him. Twice he started to sit up, reaching for her as he groaned with desire, and she pushed him back.

"Wait, Tony, wait, so much more. It has been a long, long time."

The third time she started to urge him to wait, he rolled her on the bed and stretched out beside her to pull her into his arms and kiss her hungrily.

His tongue went deep, his arms banding her. As his fingers tangled in her hair, he kissed her possessively.

"I want you," she whispered, meaning it with all her being, holding back a declaration of love, yet knowing she was hopelessly lost.

He moved between her legs to kiss her, driving her beyond thought, until desire became an aching torment.

"Tony," she whispered.

"Say it. You want me to love you," he commanded in her ear, his breath warm, his tongue hot and wet.

"Yes," she replied, meaning more than he could ever know. Running one hand over him, she held him tightly as she kissed him, moaning softly.

Finally, he paused, his fingers in her hair again. "Do you have protection?"

"No," she whispered. "I'm not on anything."

He moved away to find his slacks on the floor and return with a packet. She watched as he got a condom.

His gaze roamed over her and then he came down to hold her, his arms going around her while he kissed her. "Ah, Isabelle, I've wanted you more than you can ever guess. I never forgot and now I wonder why I didn't pursue seeing you no matter what interfered."

"Doesn't matter now," she whispered, for the moment feeling a bond with him that deep inside she knew was pure illusion. "This moment is what matters. You're in my arms." She pulled him close to kiss him again and he entered her slowly, the brief pain transforming as he filled her and moved.

She arched her back, meeting him, feeling one with him, warm, body against body, each held tightly while they kissed and loved intimately, a union that momentarily transcended reality.

Tension heightened, his control lasting as he pleasured her and she made love to him in return, carrying them higher and higher until they crashed over a summit, a spectacular climax that exploded with blinding lights behind her closed eyes and a roaring in her ears that had to be her own pounding heartbeat.

She held him tightly, imagining her hold on him would last, that the intimacy they had just shared would last even though she knew better.

"This is a special night, Tony," she whispered, clinging tightly to him as they moved together, each gasping for breath, drifting back into the regular world.

"You're a dream come true, a man's fantasy in real life. Ah, Isabelle, seductive, enchantress, perfect."

"Foolishness, Tony. I'm definitely not perfect and I'm no enchantress. Although I'm glad you called me that because I can now tell you that you are a spellbinder, seducing and weaving magic. You are my lover, for this moment all that I want."

He kissed her and she wondered if it was to stop her chatter, to reaffirm what he had just said or simply lust. The lust that had driven them all through the weekend and all this evening. She was falling back to earth, into reality and facing what she had known all along. There was no magic, no commitment, just lust and two healthy lovers who were swept up in passion.

His kiss drove her thoughts away and she clung to him as he rolled over on his side, taking her with him, holding him as close as possible. Their legs were intertwined, and she was in his embrace, pressed tightly against him. His kisses now were sweeter, light and warm.

She hugged him, running her fingers in his thick, slightly damp curls. She refused to think beyond the present moment. Soon enough tomorrow, decisions, choices would intrude, but tonight, she was locked into this time with Tony. That's all she planned to see, think about or acknowledge.

"This is heaven," Tony murmured against her, his breath playing lightly on her temple. "I don't want to ever let you go. You are my dreams. Since I discovered who you are, you've been in my dreams every night."

She laughed softly, winding thick black curls around her fingers. "And did I live up to those dreams?"

He shifted to look at her, smiling and brushing long strands of her hair away from her face. "You more than lived up to them. Reality is far better than dreams. I told you this is perfection, heaven. Would I change anything—no. Not at the moment, anyway."

"*Not at the moment* is the key phrase," she said. "Why does this—tonight—seem so inevitable?"

"Because it was. I always knew you'd be back in my life."

"You knew no such thing," she said, smiling at him, and he grinned.

"Maybe I didn't, but once I found you, I knew you'd be back in my arms."

"That's because you've been aimed at seduction since the night you walked into my office at ten o'clock or whatever time it was."

"How could I not be with the electricity that flies between us? Ah, this has been grand, Isabelle. Move in with me."

She laughed. "Just like that. Move in with me. Tony, what a dreamer you are. Leave tomorrow out of this. Let's just have tonight and enjoy it. We'll get to tomorrow soon enough."

"Sounds like a great idea. So for now, beautiful lady, let's move to a hot tub of water and soak and talk and have a glass of wine."

"I'll accept that invitation."

"I'll carry you." He stood, picking her up in his arms. "I'll start the bath, get the wine and we're set. White, Zinfandel or red?"

"A very sweet white."

He set her on her feet in a large bathroom with a sunken tub surrounded by pots with ferns and tropical plants, some with exotic red and yellow blossoms. She watched him start the water.

As he moved around, she reached out to pick up a thick white towel and wrap it around herself.

Her gaze roamed over Tony's naked body, and desire awakened again. He turned around and she looked up to meet his gaze.

His expression changed as he looked at her. She could see desire flare to life in his brown eyes. He was aroused, walking to her, and she felt as if all the air had left the room. Her breathing became deep and labored, her heart racing. He took her into his arms to kiss her. She felt his hands, felt the towel slip away and then she was pressed against his bare, hard body, his arousal thrust against her, hard, hot, ready.

"Wait, Isabelle," he said, stepping out to retrieve a packet from a table. In seconds while she caressed him, he put on protection. Tony spread his legs, braced himself and picked her up.

"Put your legs around me," he said, lowering her on his thick staff.

She gasped with pleasure, heat suffusing her as they moved together, and she kissed his throat and neck.

"Tony, now, now," she cried, holding him tightly, surging over another brink and feeling an explosive release and climax.

She held him tightly as he shuddered and climaxed, kissing her.

He let her slide to the floor to put her feet down. She wrapped her arms around him. "Ah, Tony, that was wonderful. You are wonderful," she said.

"I'll go get us that wine," he said, leaving the room, and immediately she felt his absence.

He *was* wonderful, she thought, recalling what he had done for his sister. She wondered if the tales about him being so ruthless in business could be true when he would turn around and take such care of his younger sister.

Was Tony really ruthless? So far, he had given her a huge

promotion and let her keep the staff she wanted, giving each of them a raise. She hadn't heard anyone in Morris who had sounded disgruntled or had complaints.

So were those mere rumors about Tony? Or had he reformed? Or had his employees just not seen him do anything yet that was harsh or ruthless, but the time would come when they would see that side of him?

She wondered what was true. She liked Sydney Ryder. Could Tony be like his sister? Or was he like his father? Controlling, unethical if necessary to get what he wanted. She considered all his manipulations to get her into bed, including his enormous promotion and the salary that was almost a bribe. He had two sides and she wasn't sure which one would dominate.

In minutes he was back, placing the wineglasses on the ledge of the tub and picking her up to place her leaning back against him in the deliciously hot water.

Tony was warm, his arms around her while they talked. She could feel the vibrations in his chest against her back as he spoke of his childhood and his closeness to his sister.

"Thanks to you, it sounds as if Dylan will be my brother-in-law soon."

"I don't know whether this will get them back together. It still means your sister will be disinherited and Dylan won't be able to live with that."

"I think they both are really in love. I don't know about Dylan, but Sydney is a wreck and she doesn't need to lose another pound."

"Evidently that hasn't moved your father."

"No, it hasn't," Tony said, and a harsh note entered his voice. "I'm still shocked over what he's done. As I've said, I've never known him to do anything dishonest. I doubt if I will ever trust him as much as before."

"You were probably right about him feeling desperate over losing control of both of you. I can't imagine trying to control others. My family is so far removed from that. We've always supported each other every way we can and everyone does what he wants."

"I'll never get this family of yours straight. Tell me again."

She laughed, turning to give him a look. "Tony, you learned all the hundreds of Morris employees. You call them by name and you really know all the executives. Don't tell me my family confuses you."

"They do. That's different. When do I meet them?"

"I've decided I'll take you home to meet my family when you take me home to meet yours. Which I assume will never happen. Besides, if I took you to meet mine, they would think we're getting seriously involved with each other, with an engagement and a marriage looming. I don't think you would want to deal with that. And then, if they think you're leading me on without serious intentions, I have brothers who take a dim view of anyone messing with their sisters. If you are protective of Sydney, imagine three of you running around protecting her. It compounds," she said, smiling up at him.

"You definitely have a point. So I suppose we don't meet each other's families."

His hands went around her and he cupped her breasts, playing with her nipples, caressing her. "That's better, isn't it?"

She gasped with pleasure and closed her eyes. She ran her hands along his muscled thighs. "Tony—" she whispered, closing her eyes and becoming absorbed in touching him.

"Ah, Isabelle. Beautiful, beautiful," he whispered.

She twisted to kiss him and in minutes she moved over him, holding him tightly with her eyes closed as he caressed her. He climbed out, getting protection and pulling her into his arms to pick her up. They rocked together, climbing to a pinnacle to burst with release. She fell on him, clinging to his broad shoulders while he held her close to carry her back into the warm water.

A half hour later, she climbed out. He came up out of the

water to follow her, reaching to take her towel to slowly dry her, rubbing her from head to toe.

"Now I get to return the favor," she whispered, taking a folded towel and starting with his shoulder, running the towel over his chest and around to his back, slowly inching her way down his back and legs and then moving around in front to work her way up.

By the time she reached his upper thighs, he was aroused, hard and ready for her.

"Come here, Isabelle," he said in a deep, raspy voice. He picked her up to carry her to bed, where he held her and they made love, leisurely at first, then with abandon and finally with a desperate urgency.

"Now, I am far too exhausted to move or think," Isabelle said, sprawled on top of him, her hair spilling over his shoulder and chest.

He ran one hand through her hair while his other hand stroked her bare back. "This is good right now. Just holding you like this, close to my heart, here in my arms for the night. This is perfect."

"I agree," she said languidly, feeling as if she had melted and been poured over him. "So very handsome, Tony. You are handsome, sexy, charming."

"And you, love, are beautiful, sexy, gorgeous, burning me totally when we make love."

"I hope so," she said, smiling.

"This is grand, Isabelle. I wasn't kidding earlier. Move in with me. You want commitment. There's a commitment of sorts."

She raised an eyebrow. She would be hurt if she expected anything more from him. "Tony, moving in with you isn't a commitment in my view. I would definitely be free to move out at any time. No, I'm not moving in with you and we weren't going to talk about tomorrow yet. Not until it happens."

"Oh, sure," he said. "No tomorrows. I'd like to share today

with you. You're already here, but I'd like you to move your things in."

"Definitely not for so many reasons. Not in with you. Not you in with me. I have plans and that would not fit."

"You don't have to stay a long time. Move in for now. You'll be free to go whenever you want."

"Sorry. No. End of discussion." She rolled over beside him and he pulled her close.

"I want you, Isabelle. I don't give up easily or take no well."

"I've already discovered that much about you."

He pulled her close against him and held her. "We'll discuss this some more tomorrow," Tony said.

It was dawn before they finally stopped talking and fell asleep. Isabelle woke, stretched and looked around, turning more to look at Tony sprawled beside her. He was naked, his thick black curls tangled on his forehead. One arm was flung to one side. The sheet covered him from his hips to his feet.

Longing enveloped her as she looked at him, his chest rising and falling evenly. *Tony, I love you,* she mouthed, knowing she felt a love that wouldn't be returned. Tony had gone as far as he would go by inviting her to move in with him. She *could* do that and hope the day would come when he would decide he wanted something more lasting.

In the silence of the room, with the only sound Tony's steady breathing, she shook her head. She wanted so much more of him. She hadn't been able to resist him and had yielded to the temptation of one more magical night with him, but that's all she had ever intended it to be and all it would be.

She gazed at him, memorizing the sight of him, wanting to lean over to shower light kisses on him, certain if she did he would wake.

While she debated getting up, his arm went around her and he pulled her down, opening his eyes to focus on her. The minute she looked into his brown eyes, she saw desire that ignited her own longing.

He pulled her close against him, leaning over her to kiss her, a kiss that heightened her emotions. She wrapped her arms around him to kiss him in return and soon they were loving as if it were the first time instead of a morning after a passionate evening.

Over an hour later she called the office to say she would not be in. She made some arrangements and then broke the connection, turning to Tony, who had been kissing her nape, rubbing against her backside and fondling her breasts again.

"Tony, you need to call the office yourself. And I have to get my car. The bar will think they have an abandoned car in their lot and have it towed."

"No, they won't. I called my chauffeur last night and had him get a tow truck to take it to your house. It's done."

She rubbed her forehead. "You still haven't called the office," she said, surprised he was letting that go. "I don't even remember my calendar for today."

He snagged her wrist as she started to get out of bed. "Forget it. You made your call and you were efficient and if I had been on the other end of the line, I wouldn't have suspected a thing."

"Call the office. You're shameless."

He grinned and she had to laugh. He swooped over her and pushed her onto the bed to kiss her thoroughly. In minutes she held him tightly, forgetting about the office and phone calls and any demands besides Tony's mouth and hands.

Hours later, Tony opened his eyes. Bright sunlight streamed into the room. He turned to look at Isabelle, who slept beside him. The sheet covered her to her shoulders. She lay on her side, facing him, one arm flung out across him, her silky blond hair fanned over the pillow and her shoulder and back, partially spilling over her face. He carefully combed it back from her face to look at her profile. He hadn't told her she was the first woman he had ever asked to move in with him. He had moved in with a couple of women in his life, but the relationships hadn't lasted and he had never expected them to. If he was the one to move in, he could move out when he so desired. By asking Isabelle to move in with him, he was offering an intimate arrangement, but it was far from offering marriage.

It wouldn't be lasting with Isabelle, either. He wasn't ready for commitment and that hadn't changed. He felt driven to make billionaire while he was relatively young. It kept his father from meddling. It would give him all he wanted the rest of his life and he could take care of Sydney if he needed to. Any one of those reasons was enough to avoid a serious relationship for years longer.

At the same time, he wanted Isabelle in his life more than he had ever wanted any other woman. She would never ask him to move in with her, so he had to ask her. This was the only possible way to get her into his arms most nights. She was the most enticing, exciting woman he had ever known. He had let her slip out of his life once before. He didn't intend to let that happen again for a long time. Would he be able to hold her? Would she stay if he couldn't offer marriage?

He had never asked himself that question concerning a woman before. It had always been easy—the question not as important to him. Isabelle was different. The realization of how much she had wound herself into his life and how badly he wanted her around, shocked him. He wasn't in love. He couldn't be. He had guarded against that happening because he intended to reach his goals. Love wasn't something that happened to him and he would know if it did. He had always been certain no one could fall in love against their own wishes. If she just weren't so damned independent and had a goal of marriage by thirty. What woman in today's world had a goal like that? Maybe more than he realized, because most of them probably wouldn't tell. Could he think about extending his goal just a few years? Was it worth losing her to stubbornly stick to his original plan? To his disgust, that inability to yield or adjust did sound like his father's influence and genes.

Tony looked at her, her flawless skin and long, pale lashes, her rosy mouth, the cascade of gorgeous hair that always captivated him. When desire stirred, he was torn between wanting to just look at her and making love to her. He didn't think he would ever tire of gazing at her.

He wanted her to live with him and she wasn't going to. He could feel the resolve behind her refusal. "Gorgeous woman," he whispered, "I want you with me." He pulled the sheet to her waist and drew a deep breath. Heat suffused him, and he was rampant with desire as he trailed his hand over her breasts and watched her stir.

He bent to kiss her. Her arm wound around his neck. Her blue eyes gazed up at him, sleep filled, coming awake, desire igniting. She was warm, relaxed, naked. He kissed her, caressing her and relishing rediscovery, wanting to stretch the day into days with her.

It was the middle of the afternoon before she sat in the bed with a sheet wrapped around her while she braided her hair. "Tony, I need to dress and go home."

He lay with his hands behind his head, watching her. "I vote no to that one. Stay tonight. The day is gone, anyway, so why not?"

"Why not, indeed. Tony, this is sinful. We have been making love since last night. That's just plain decadent."

"Delightful, you mean. Stay now. I'll cook dinner tonight. I haven't shown you my house." His cell phone buzzed, and she was grateful for the interruption in his attempts at persuasion.

"While you take that call, I'm going to shower."

Rolling over, he stretched out his arm to pick up his cell phone from the floor.

"Wait a minute. I have a text from Sydney." He punched buttons, scanned his message quickly and set the phone on the bedside table. "She's made up with Dylan."

"Great for both of them!" Isabelle exclaimed, smiling broadly. "I'm so very glad."

He pulled her into his arms, holding her against his chest. "You're the reason they're together. Otherwise, my dad would have gotten away with his ploy. See what you already mean to me and my sister."

"I didn't do that much. Just told you the truth about Dylan. He did the rest. I'm so glad. I was shocked when I saw how thin and pale and miserable they both were."

"Being in love takes a toll."

"You say that as if it's something frightful."

"They're wrecks. At least, I'm taking your word for it about Dylan's appearance."

"It isn't because they're in love. It's because they're having a rough time not being free to love each other. It's the interference that has them wrecks, not their love."

"That they're together again is very good news. I felt a little guilt because I was the one who told Dad that Dylan had stopped seeing her because he didn't want her to lose her inheritance. If Dad hadn't known that, he could never have told Sydney what he did."

"You never dreamed how he would use the information. Also, I'm glad you're happy they're together. It will mean she will lose her inheritance and that you'll put her through medical school."

He shrugged. "If she's happy, then so am I. I have the money for her schooling. I'll never miss it."

"Don't make me admire you."

He smiled. "Why not? Want to tell yourself I'm an ogre?"

"Hardly. I know you're a workaholic through and through."

"Not quite so through and through," he said, picking up his

cell phone and tossing it to her. She glanced at it and raised her eyebrows questioningly.

"I've just turned it off. Texted the office that I'm not taking calls unless the place burns down."

Surprised, she looked at the phone in her hand to see it was silenced. "You can still get text messages."

"Right, but they're not so intrusive and when I saw that was from Sydney, I thought it would be of interest to you, too. See, I can let go of work sometimes."

"Sometimes, Tony, but it's rare, not routine," she said, unimpressed because it was a temporary fix. Work was ingrained in Tony the same as breathing and sleeping.

"Yes, that's right. I wouldn't have gotten where I am if I hadn't given my full attention to business. Enough on that subject." Tony pulled her close and waved his hand. "I'll give you a tour of the house. This is my bedroom and you've seen my bathroom."

Still thinking about his workaholic ethic, she looked at the bedroom that was large enough to hold her entire condo. "I'm amazed this room is so huge. For that matter, so is your bathroom, although you may have had it redone."

"This is all new. It looks the same age as the original part because I told them to keep it that way—I love the big windows, the high ceilings and wood trim. I have a gym in a separate building. There's a pool and I have a theater room, a billiard room, plus the usual rooms. I think you'd like it here." He rolled over, wrapping his arm around her waist. "I meant it. I want you with me."

With her heartbeat quickening, she gazed into his dark eyes. How persuasive and tempting he was, yet how disastrous it would be for her future. The charismatic, handsome man came with guaranteed heartaches if she became closely involved.

Nine

Incredibly tempted, wanting to say yes, she gazed into his dark brown eyes. "Tony—"

He placed his index finger lightly on her lips, stopping her reply. "Consider living here. Don't give me an answer yet one way or another. I want you to be sure. Just think it through. This is a nice place to live. I hope I'm a nice guy to live with."

Smiling, she ran her fingers through his hair. "I'm sure you're a nice guy to live with. You're definitely a sexy guy to go to bed with," she added in a sultry voice, and watched his expression change, his eyes growing darker with desire.

"I want you here with me," he whispered, magic words that thrilled and tantalized her. The temptation was huge, alluring, filled with promises of so many wonderful moments, fulfillment, excitement, a real possibility of Tony falling in love. Was it worth the risks to have a relationship with him? "I've never asked a woman to move in with me. You're special, Isabelle."

She drew a deep breath. His words thrilled her. One more reason that made it definitely worth the risks to see him more.

Was he falling in love with her? Real love that would bind his heart to her?

She wanted to tell him yes, take the chance on a full-blown affair so that he would fall deeply in love, deeply enough that he would want to marry. Definitely enough to continue seeing him no matter what the consequences. Moving in with him took more thought. The acceptance was on the tip of her tongue, yet the reasons to refuse were strong enough to keep her silent.

He kissed her, pulling her into his arms, her shower forgotten.

It was six the next morning when he drove her home and walked her to her door.

"I have to leave town today. Go out with me Friday night when I return," he said.

She nodded. "Thank you. That would be nice," she answered, standing on tiptoe and wrapping her arms around his neck to kiss him. Maybe Tony was falling in love whether he realized it or not. There was far more chance of it happening if she remained in his life than if she didn't.

Instantly, he kissed her passionately in return.

Minutes later, she ended the kiss. "I'll see you Friday." She went inside, feeling as if it had been a lifetime since she had left home.

Her life had changed and she was caught in the throes of dealing with Tony in all the intimate ways she had intended to avoid. Now she faced the question of the future and whether or not to move in with him. If she didn't, would he continue their relationship?

She decided to go in late to work while she pondered giving Tony an answer. She wouldn't be able to concentrate on her job this morning, anyway. Weighing the possibilities, she always came out wanting more than being a live-in.

At noon she went to the office and attempted to keep her attention on work, finding her thoughts drifting easily. Relieved that Tony had had to leave town, she went home that night to solitude, a quiet night to think things through.

Memories were a torment. She had had a wonderful time with him. His home was beautiful. Tony was sexy, marvelous, handsome—so many great things. She was in love even though she had tried to avoid it. He wanted her, no question there, but how lasting would it be without commitment?

Thursday, she worked out with Jada, opening up to her good friend about the dilemma and coming no closer to a resolution. She missed Tony and wanted to be with him. He had called every night, talking with her more than two hours each time yet never mentioning his offer.

When he called Thursday night she was settled in bed, knowing she would be on the phone a long time.

"I really miss you," he said in a voice that made her heartbeat speed up as much as if he had just walked into the room.

"I miss you, too, Tony," she admitted.

"If it's all right with you, I may change our Friday night plans slightly," he said. "Sydney called me. She and Dylan want to take us to dinner Friday night. I think this is a gesture of gratitude for what you did."

"That's fine," she said, relieved for the young couple. "So they're together."

"Yes, and she sounded happy. I haven't talked to Dad yet. Neither has Sydney. She said she wanted to get her life straightened out with Dylan and when the time is right, she'll tell Dad. She's busy, has her own apartment, so she doesn't see them often. She may be holding back, partially for the same reason I am. I need to get some distance from what happened so I can hang on to my temper with him. Enough about that. Where are you now?"

"In bed," she replied, smiling.

He groaned. "I want to cut this trip short and come home now, but I can't. I don't think we'll be with Sydney and Dylan late Friday. I hope not. I feel I've been away from you a month instead of a few days."

Her heart warmed and she smiled. "I feel the same way." Cautious not to read too much into what he said, she changed the topic to business. "How's the deal going that you're working on?" She listened while he talked at length about the small chain of hotels in Missouri, Arkansas and Louisiana he was thinking about acquiring.

Their conversation moved on when he asked about her work, things at the office. It was after two in the morning before they parted. The calls were getting lengthier and they had more to share.

If she moved in with him, would he fall in love? That was the burning question she kept asking herself. Could she stand to refuse him? Because if she did, she expected him to move out of her life again, just as he had done in the past.

She was on the verge of deciding yes repeatedly, but each time, obstacles arose. If she lived with him, she wouldn't be able to find someone who shared her desire to marry and have a family. Also, if she moved in with Tony, she had to face what it might be like three years from now when she was still waiting for him to fall in love. Or much sooner, if he broke it off. She could be brokenhearted now, but nothing compared to living with him and then having him walk out of her life.

Friday night, as she changed into a bright red crepe dress, she still didn't have a final answer to give Tony. Her heart argued to move in—wisdom cried no. When she opened the door to face Tony, her heart thudded. She had a fleeting awareness of how handsome he was in his navy suit. He stepped inside, reaching for her and kicking the door closed behind him. He wrapped her in his arms, kissing her as she held him tightly and kissed him in return.

Time ceased to exist until she remembered their dinner engagement. "Tony, we have to go."

He released her slightly, "I don't want to go anywhere else. I want to be alone with you." His voice was deeper than usual.

"I know, but we told Dylan and Sydney we would. It won't be a late evening."

"No, it won't," he said. "Let's get this over with."

As they hurried to the waiting limousine, neither brought up the question that had dominated her thoughts all week. She still was undecided, tempted to accept yet always facing solid reasons to say no.

As soon as Tony sat beside her in the limo, he pulled her close to kiss her again.

When they walked into the lobby of the luxurious restaurant, Dylan and Sydney waited. The moment she saw Sydney, Isabelle was relieved. Both Sydney and Dylan looked radiant.

"There they are," she said.

"They look like *afters* in before and after pictures. Thankfully," Tony said quietly to her, and then gave his sister a light hug. "Sydney, you look pretty and, frankly, far better than the last time I saw you." He turned to shake hands with Dylan.

Sydney hugged Isabelle, smiling at her. "I'm grateful to you," Sydney said. "To both of you," she added, glancing between Isabelle and Tony. "That's why we wanted to take you to dinner."

The moment they were seated at a linen-covered table and had given drink orders, Dylan turned to Tony and Isabelle. "We have several things to tell you both. First, this dinner is a token thank-you for revealing what had really happened."

"It's impossible to tell you how grateful we are to you," Sydney added, her brown eyes sparkling.

"We're together again because of you," Dylan continued. "That's one reason for this dinner. There's another." He paused to hold Sydney's right hand. "I've asked Sydney to marry me and she's accepted."

Smiling broadly, Sydney held out her left hand and a diamond sparkled in the candlelight. "Congratulations!" Isabelle and Tony spoke at the same time.

Isabelle felt a lurch as Sydney turned slightly to Dylan. The look they exchanged plainly expressed their love as much as if they had verbally declared it. Suddenly, she knew what her answer had to be to Tony.

She looked at a beautiful emerald-cut diamond surrounded by smaller diamonds on a wide gold band. "It's beautiful, Sydney, and I'm thrilled for both of you," Isabelle said, meaning it. "Dylan, this is wonderful news. Both of you look incredibly happy."

"We are," he said quietly to Sydney, for a moment his smile faltering. "Whatever the consequences, this is what we've decided to do. Sydney convinced me to marry her," he added teasingly.

Tony reached out to hug Sydney's neck, a light, brotherly embrace. "I'll give you back the check, Syd. I meant what I said about putting you through medical school."

Dylan shook his head. "Tony, we'll be married. I'll send her to med school."

Tony shook his head. "I want to do this as a wedding gift to both of you. Also, Dylan, I have to admit, I'm enjoying my freedom from being hassled by Dad and this is a little bit of payback for what he's done. Let me do this."

Sydney grasped Dylan's arm. "Let him, Dylan. You'll never understand about our father and how he's tried to control our lives."

"No, I don't understand. I'm sure Isabelle doesn't, either. I've heard her talk about her family." He looked at Tony. "Very well, that's an enormous, marvelous wedding present and we both appreciate it," he said, glancing at Sydney, who smiled at him.

"Is a date set?" Isabelle asked.

"We're talking about it," Dylan replied.

"Probably around June. Something small with close friends, and whatever family will be there," Sydney added, her smile fading. "I don't expect Mom or Dad to attend. If they don't, Tony, will you give the bride away?"

"I'd be honored, Syd. If Dad appears, fine. He can do the honor. Have you told him yet?" Tony asked.

"No. I want to wait until Dylan and I have our plans made and I'm not so emotional and angry over it. I'll tell Mom and Dad soon."

"Syd, I don't want to say anything to them until you have," Tony said.

"I'll let you know."

They paused while champagne was opened. Through toasts and through dinner, Isabelle tried to join in Dylan's and Sydney's obvious happiness, but underneath her smiles was a steady hurt. She was glad for them. Their love was unmistakable.

When the evening finally ended as they parted with Dylan and Sydney, Sydney hugged Isabelle again. "Thank you so much. I wouldn't have Dylan back if it weren't for you. Be patient with my brother. He's really a good guy at heart."

Isabelle smiled. "I'll remember your advice," she said, continuing to wonder about the depth of Tony's objectives.

She looked into the female version of Tony, dark brown eyes identical to his, a mop of thick black curls, longer than Tony's. How well did Isabelle really know her brother? Did she have any idea of his ambition to be a billionaire by forty?

"I'm happy for you and I'm glad the two of you are together again. You appear to have truly found love, an elusive commodity it seems."

Dylan turned to put his arm around Sydney's waist, pulling her close against him. "Thanks to both of you again."

"Thank *you* for dinner," Isabelle said, while Tony said the same. The limo pulled up and the chauffeur held the door. They climbed inside and Tony turned to her, pulling her into his arms.

Isabelle came willingly, hungry for his kisses, wanting to love him, wishing she could bind him to her, overcome the force that drove him to put business and success first over all else. "How I want you," he whispered, kissing her again before she could answer him. She held him tightly, kissing him, taking and giving, knowing it was fleeting, meaningless to him.

She lost track of time, but all too soon the limo stopped. "We're at your place, Isabelle. Come home with me tonight. I'll see you home in the morning, but come back with me now."

She nodded and was in his embrace again.

At his house, he released her and they stepped out of the limo to go in through a side door. The minute they were in the mansion, Tony drew her into his arms.

Clothes were strewn all the way to a downstairs bedroom. She glimpsed a four-poster bed, lots of pillows, white furniture. Little else registered with her. She was in Tony's magical embrace again.

They loved through the night and fell asleep in each other's arms. Isabelle was the last to go to sleep. On her side and held close by Tony, she ran her fingers in his hair and then along his jaw, studying him, memorizing his features. "Tonight was special, Tony," she whispered, knowing he was asleep and would never hear her or know. "I love you."

She could not think about *if only* possibilities. She had to accept Tony the way he was and face reality. She studied him as he slept, her heart filled with love and longing. How could ambition so blind him to what was wonderful in life?

Sleep would not come. Speculation was futile. She refused to think about the future and tried to cling to this night, this hour with Tony beside her, one arm holding her close. No one could predict tomorrow.

When she stirred hours later, Tony leaned over to kiss her. Instantly her arms circled his neck and they made love until sunshine spilled into the room over an hour later.

"I'll ask again, Isabelle, will you come and live here with me?"

She sat up, pulling a top sheet close around her, shaking her long hair away from her face, knowing the moment for decision had come. "No, I won't," she answered. "I would love to, Tony, but I want more than I'll get by just moving into your house."

"You want love. Take a chance, move in and see what happens. It's great right now. I would expect it to get even better."

Saddened, hurting, wishing he would set business on a back burner, give it second place in his life and propose, she knew that wouldn't happen. Not until after forty and he had achieved billionaire would his goals change. Business came first.

She sat close to him, the sheet pulled beneath her arms while he had it across his lap. His chest was bare, tempting even after a night of love. She felt as if she were breaking to pieces inside. "Tony, I want it all. I want what Sydney has—commitment. Even more, I want what my parents have, a long, steady love. That's what I've always wanted."

"Live with me. It may turn into love and then into marriage," he said, caressing her nape, playing with her hair.

May. She shook her head. "I want to say yes, but I have to say no. I saw the love between Dylan and Sydney. I want that. I want commitment, your love. I want to be first in someone's life, not to follow a goal to become a billionaire by forty. You might fall in love and you might marry, but you won't give up your driving goals to achieve that billionaire status. And that means putting work ahead of all else. No thanks. That isn't what I want. I'm not sitting home alone week after week, raising children without a father, watching you think about deals instead of your family. You and I have vastly different goals and views of what's important. You pursue yours and I hope you get them and I hope they make you happy. I'll pursue mine."

"You're presuming the worst, envisioning a scenario that

might not happen. Half the world is filled with men and women who don't spend every waking hour together, but they love each other and love their families and raise fine children."

"True, but I've watched my best friend's father, who was a workaholic. They barely saw him and he missed too many big events in his children's lives. It's not spending every waking hour together. It's putting the other person first in your life and the two of you together being more important than business. It's a true partner in the family to help with kids and grow old together. That's the kind of love your sister has with Dylan and you can see it just by looking at them. I'm not moving in with you. Now's the time for the break before my heart is shattered so badly, I'd never recover."

"That's ridiculous. You'll recover from a broken heart if you ever have one, but that isn't what I intend to have happen when you move in with me."

His eyes darkened and a muscle worked in his jaw. She hurt all over, but she was going to stand firm with her decision because she thought any other way would lead to far greater heartache.

"It's been wonderful, Tony. You know I'm in love with you now—"

Tony reached for her.

"Isabelle, come here," he said, his arm circling her waist.

She gripped his wrist and removed his arm. "Just wait and listen. I love you, but I will get over this because we haven' bound our lives together yet."

"Then take a chance on us, dammit," he said, clasping her shoulder with his hand. "Give us some time together and try to see what develops and how deep it goes."

She shook her head again. "No. I already know how deep my love for you goes. I want it all. I watched Dylan and Sydney tonight. They have it. Each one is first in the other's life. They're deeply in love and there were moments when the outside world didn't exist for them. They were barely with us some of the time. There's a unity between them that is a strong bond. That's the kind of love I want. I'm glad they've found it, because I think it's both special and rare."

"Isabelle, dammit, stop. Give us some time together. Two weeks. See if you feel the same after that. You're not giving us a chance. You've got all these preconceived notions. I won't be like your friend's father. Give us a fair chance at this and then stop and take a long look and make a monumental, life-changing decision when you have more knowledge about what you're doing."

"Mr. Logic," she said, fighting back tears. "No, Tony. I already know. You won't change. You can't change. If you'd had any intention of changing, you would have proposed marriage instead of asking me to move in with you. I'm going to dress and I want to go home. You can send the limo to deposit me at home and you don't even have to ride along."

"To hell with this," he said. He pulled her into his embrace, kissing her passionately. She was stiff, unresponsive, but his mouth worked magic and in seconds she kissed him in return.

Her heart pounded and she held him tightly, kissing him, wanting to kiss him into agreement with her, hoping he would never forget her. She loved him and she let it show through her kisses and responses.

He groaned, wanting her, making love furiously, hungrily, while she returned it as passionately, her hands roaming over him.

She leaned back to frame his face with her hands. "I love you, Tony. It might not be marriage with me, but someday, you'll wed someone. You're going to miss the most wonderful part of life while you're out chasing money. You're capable of so much." She kissed him long, slowly, passionately.

He held her tightly, wrapping his arms around her, bending

over her to kiss her as if it were the last kiss he could ever have from any woman. "Damn, I want you, Isabelle."

"And I want your love. There is a difference, Tony." She slipped free and hurried to gather her clothes and leave the room, determined to find a shower away from Tony's seductive kisses.

Tears stung her eyes because it was over between them. She could feel that to her toes and she had seen the look in his dark eyes—anger, hurt, refusal. She hoped he wouldn't accompany her on the ride home. It was over between them and the sooner the break came, the better off they both would be.

She showered, letting her tears flow freely, wiping her eyes as she dried and hung up the towel. She dressed swiftly, rebraiding her hair and dreading confronting him to ask for a ride home.

When she found him, he was in the library. He had dressed in charcoal trousers and his white dress shirt.

"You don't have to come along."

"Don't be ridiculous," he said, smiling at her as if nothing had happened between them. "I brought you here and I'll see you home." He draped his arm across her shoulders.

They rode home in silence and at her door, he pulled her to him for a brief kiss.

"Would it matter if I had told you that I'm in love with you?" he asked.

"Now we won't know, will we? You didn't say you were and you're still not," she replied.

"I know I'm going to miss you like hell," he said, grinding out the words. He kissed her one long, passionate last time and then turned to hurry back to his limo.

"Goodbye, Tony," she whispered, knowing she had lost him now, but that had been her intention. She hurried inside, locking the door and running to her bedroom. She flung herself across the bed to cry. She wanted Tony, wanted to be part of his life, wanted his lovemaking, his laughter, his drive. Instead, she had told him goodbye and he was out of her life.

* * *

The weekend was silent and miserable. She exercised twice as long as usual and tried to do work she had brought home from the office, but her concentration was poor.

Monday morning, she cried silently as she moved through the condo, hunting for clothes to wear to work, knowing she should pick her best to give the image of confidence.

She made it in to work twenty minutes early and headed straight to her office, hoping she would see very few people the whole day. Tony was out of her life and she should start getting ready for it.

How easy that should be, but that wasn't the case.

The day seemed three times longer than normal, the hours dragging, her mind wandering from business.

The worst moments were the meetings, the times she would pass Tony somewhere, the meetings when he was included. The next day was worse and she decided the pain was not worth the promotion, the pay, the move up in her career. Feeling as if she would never be able to concentrate, she called Vernon Irwin to see if his offer for a job with his company was still valid.

The following Monday morning, the sixth of March, she tendered her resignation, putting a letter in a manila envelope and leaving it for Tony's secretary before he arrived at work.

At nine his secretary called to make an appointment for a meeting with Tony.

Isabelle dreaded the meeting, yet it had to happen. She was losing sleep, wondering whether she would look as much a wreck as Sydney Ryder had.

At three, she headed to Tony's office. The moment she stepped inside, her heart thudded when she looked into his eyes.

Ten

He came around his desk and motioned toward an empty leather chair. "Have a seat."

He held her resignation letter in his hand. "I read this, Isabelle. I'm disappointed. Whatever there is—was—between us, I hoped we could keep our personal lives separate from work. I made you a fantastic offer, gave you a promotion, which has enabled you to secure an offer like this from Irwin."

A muscle worked in his jaw and his eyes blazed with anger, yet she could still see desire. She suspected if she told him to tear up the letter and she would move in, it would clear everything instantly. She was still tempted to do so. She wanted to walk into his arms and kiss him, be held and to love him for hours, as they had done not so long ago.

"Why?" he asked.

"I can't work around you. I can't keep my mind on my work. I can't focus. I can't think about the job because I miss you. I remember moments with you, shared laughter, our long phone calls. I miss you every hour of the day and the nights are far worse. I can't stop thinking about when we were together. I can't stop missing you. You asked and there it is."

"Damn," he snapped. "Why are you doing this to yourself and to both of us? Maybe I'm falling in love. You're jumping to conclusions about a future that you really know nothing about. Nobody knows the future."

"I may be, Tony. But this is what I have to do. I haven't changed and neither have you. I want marriage to a man dedicated to his family. I want his main goal in life to be his family—the kids he raises, his marriage. Go make your billions. I want simpler things. I want to love a man who loves me in return and who loves his kids and puts us all first in his life."

"How can you do that and say you're in love with me? Why are you doing this to us? Ambition isn't a sin. Most women would welcome that I'm hardworking and successful. Since when are those two qualities bad?"

"They're wonderful qualities in the right perspective. When they dominate all else, including your love for your family, that's when it's out of balance. That's what I don't want any part of. I've seen what it does to a family. Sorry, Tony."

"Dammit, Isabelle." He pulled her close to kiss her hard and long. She returned his kiss, lost in passion, crying, torn by conflicting emotions of love and loss. He released her abruptly. She opened her eyes slowly to watch him studying her.

"You're crying. You kiss with passion that sets me ablaze. You've told me you love me. Stop fighting what you know you want with all your being."

"I will not. I know what the price might be."

"All right, Isabelle. Take the new job. Go your own way. You don't want me in your life, go find happiness somewhere else," he snapped, striding past her to open his office door and hold it, waiting for her to exit.

She drew a deep breath and left his office, knowing she was walking out of his life.

She wanted him right now even with the harsh words. He was hurt and angry, totally unaccustomed to defeat or rejection. Tears threatened and she wanted out of the office, away from people she worked with, away from Tony.

She hurt all over. She had resigned from a wonderful job. Told Tony she didn't want to continue seeing him. She loved him and those actions hurt, yet she was certain she had taken the only course she could live with. She remembered all the times her friend had bitterly complained about the absence of her father. She didn't want that for herself or her children and she knew she would never be happy with that kind of life and taking a role secondary to Tony's success in business. To become a billionaire in the next few years would take intense dedication. Some women could accept that kind of life. Some preferred it. She didn't. It was personal preference and she had made her decision.

She stepped outside, gulping air, letting the tears come as she rushed to her car to climb inside.

Driving home, she tried to stop thinking about Tony and keep her mind on her driving.

Finally, she was in the haven of her condo. She threw herself on her sofa to cry, trying to give vent to the hurt and hoping she could pour it out and get over it and get over him. Better now than later.

She wondered whether he really cared and how long it would take him to forget her.

She made plans to take some time between jobs to regain her composure. She couldn't start a new job in the state she was in at present because her concentration was gone. She had asked Irwin for time and she decided now to get out of Dallas, far away, with a change of scenery and try to get her emotions under control and adjust to telling Tony goodbye.

Her family knew a little about her problems and the new job and they were hovering over her with good intentions, but she wanted some time alone. Her condo and plants would be fine for a week.

After searching through brochures and talking to a travel agent, she flew to Alabama because of the attractive beach resort the travel agent found. Isabelle rented a small house on the Gulf where she could have solitude and try to get over Tony, wondering if she ever would in a lifetime. She could imagine he would throw himself into work until another woman interested him.

For the next few weeks Tony poured himself into work, traveling and spending the rest of March away from Dallas. The more time that passed, the more he missed Isabelle. The first week of April on a Sunday afternoon he received a text from Sydney telling him that she had seen their parents, who were furious with her. He asked Sydney to come by if she had time, and in an hour she was at his house.

"Come in, Syd. You look great," he said, meaning it. His sister had regained some weight. Her cheeks were rosy and, to his relief, she looked radiantly happy.

"Thanks, Tony. You don't look so hot yourself. Are you sick?"

"No, I'm not sick. Just busy," he snapped, growing more annoyed with each person who asked how he was feeling or told him he looked as if he had caught something. "Whatever Dad and Mom said, you don't look as if it's crushed you."

"I love Dylan and they're not taking that from me again," she replied.

"Let's sit in the family room."

"I can't stay. I'm meeting Dylan, but I wanted to stop by and tell you about seeing Mom and Dad."

"So is Dad still threatening all the same things?"

"Yes, and he's angry that we've learned the truth about what he did. Actually, I think he's embarrassed that he got caught."

Tony shook his head. "He's angry that we learned the truth," he repeated. "He should be apologizing all over the place for what he did and trying to make it up to you."

She nodded. "I thought so, too. He didn't like getting caught. Mom is angry about Dylan, saying I'll never be happy. I'm not marrying someone to please them. Anyway, thank you again for your huge gift to us. We'll get along without the inheritance. That doesn't matter as much to me."

"I don't know that I can understand or agree, but I want you to be happy. You know if I ever do inherit, I'll share it with you."

She smiled at him. "That's the future, Tony. I wouldn't be concerned with it now. You can't possibly guess what will happen."

"True. I haven't talked to Dad yet. I don't think I should until I can cool down enough to hang on to my temper."

"He's probably embarrassed to see you. He knows he's lost some respect from both of us even though he won't acknowledge it. He told me he tried to get Dylan out of my life for my own good and that later I would thank him."

"Damn, Sydney, of all my friends' fathers who were so interfering and controlling, I think Dad turned out to be the worst for his actions with you."

"I doubt if I'll see much of them for a while."

"Can't blame you. They brought that on themselves."

"I need to go, Tony. I just wanted to let you know. You've made the break so much easier for me."

He stepped outside to walk with her to her car and held the door for her while she slid behind the wheel. "I'm glad I can. And I'm glad you're back with Dylan, if that makes you happy," he said, thinking about Isabelle and feeling a knot of anger and loss.

"Hopefully, they won't try to interfere with you seeing Isabelle."

"No problem there. Isabelle and I aren't seeing each other, anyway."

Sydney frowned. "None of my business, but I'm sorry because I liked her a lot. I thought maybe you did, too."

"Isabelle wants to get married. That's not in my agenda."

Sydney smiled. "Ah, my stubborn brother. Well, as long as you're happy and don't miss her, okay." Her eyes narrowed and she slanted her head. "Tony, is that why you look as if you've had a case of the flu? Because Isabelle is gone and you don't want her to be?"

"Sydney, I've been working," he said in a clipped tone, wishing he could sound more casual and less annoyed. "Don't start on me."

She studied him. "You're my brother and I love you, but you can really be mule-stubborn sometimes. You don't look happy."

"Tell Dylan hello for me." He closed the car door and she started the engine.

"All right. I'll be quiet. Now that I know Isabelle has walked out, to me you do look like a man in love. I'm going," she added hastily, revving the engine.

Relieved, he stepped away from her car.

He watched her drive away. Thinking about Isabelle, he returned to the house to continue working. Annoyed by Sydney's remarks, he walked along the hall with his thoughts on Isabelle. He hated to admit it even to himself, but he missed her more each day instead of less and he hadn't expected that to happen.

Marriage? It was impossible to lose sight of his goals. Marriage definitely wasn't in his best interest. If he didn't acquire more wealth and power, he would be back fighting with his father over every big issue in his life.

"Dammit," he said. Sydney hadn't made him feel better. He was glad she was happy, but he didn't need to hear he looked like he had the flu.

When he walked into his office his attention went to the phone on his desk. He wanted to reach for it and call Isabelle.

He shook his head. He needed to get a grip and focus completely on his goal and the business at hand.

Within the hour he gave up and went to his room to change for a run, hoping to shake thoughts of Isabelle and lose himself in physical activity, reassuring himself that within weeks he wouldn't care that she was out of his life.

Isabelle was busy in her new job. She still hurt and missed Tony badly. Whenever she saw a tall man with black curly hair, her heart thudded and she had to look twice to convince herself it was not Tony.

Tralear Hotels had just bought out another hotel chain. They had built a new seven-story office building and Isabelle was instantly busy and working overtime to get brochures, invitations and the graphic art work done for their grand opening reception and celebration. Isabelle was thankful to be constantly busy, hoping all the work would distract her from her misery.

One afternoon when she was getting a haircut, she picked up a local magazine to see Tony's picture and an article about a contribution his family was making to a local museum. Her heart missed a beat as she looked at his picture. So familiar, yet far out of her life.

It was a Ryder contribution, so she wondered whether he had made up with his father since the family was making the donation.

Two nights later, she received a phone call from Sydney Ryder. Tears stung Isabelle's eyes as she heard Sydney's voice.

"I hear you have a new job."

"Yes, I do."

"Congratulations! Guess you didn't like working for my brother."

"That wasn't it, Sydney."

"I called because we've set a date of June twenty-third. We'll have a destination wedding at Grand Cayman. I would love for you to be a bridesmaid."

"Sydney, thank you. I'm honored you asked me," Isabelle said, feeling caught in a real dilemma. "I would love to, but things weren't so good between your brother and me when we parted. I don't want to bring any tension to the wedding at a time that should be joyful. I think if you want harmony and a wonderful time by all, you'll look elsewhere for your bridesmaid."

"I'm sorry, Isabelle. Tony told me, but I didn't know it was a really bad breakup, although he looked terrible when I saw him and he was as grouchy as a bear."

Shocked, Isabelle's eyes widened as she tried to imagine Tony fitting such a description and wondered whether a business deal had gone sour, because she couldn't imagine he had been snarly over their breakup. She tried to pay attention to Sydney. "I really wanted people who are important to me to be in our wedding party."

"That's sweet and I do thank you. I know it's best I decline."

"I understand. I'm annoyed with my woodenheaded brother about this, but I still love you both. Come to the wedding if you can. I'm really sorry. I was so in hopes that Tony was falling in love, which he looks as if he did, but Tony wouldn't recognize falling in love if it bit him. He'd be better off."

"Your brother can certainly take care of himself. Don't start worrying about us now."

"I like you, Isabelle, and I think you were good for Tony. I just hate to see him lose you."

"He knows what he wants. Thank you, Sydney, for asking me. I'm really pleased that you did, but that's a time when everyone should share in your joy."

"Just stay a friend. I'll hear about you and see you sometimes with Dylan."

"I'm so happy for both of you," Isabelle said, thinking about

Tony and feeling as if her loss was growing instead of diminishing as she puzzled over Sydney's description of him.

"Thanks, Isabelle. I hope you get over Tony quickly so you don't even care if he's around or not by the time of our wedding."

"Hopefully, I will," she said. "Thanks, again."

They ended the call and Isabelle cried quietly, missing Tony, knowing she was going to regret her decision for a long time to come. He could be seeing another woman. His bad disposition could be due purely to business. Looking terrible—she couldn't imagine that and guessed Sydney had a different view of her brother than the rest of the female world. Had Tony stopped thinking about her? Only time would tell.

Another week passed and Tony piled on work, knowing that would be his salvation. Always, he had been able turn off his private life and concentrate on the business at hand. Now he found memories of Isabelle were intruding at all hours of each day. He could no longer go to meetings and concentrate on the speaker. Too many times, his thoughts drifted. He wondered what Isabelle was doing. Where was she? Did she miss him as much as he missed her?

He focused on the speaker, following the tables of figures being presented, until he realized his mind had wandered again. Clenching his fist, he tried to concentrate, wishing the meeting would end quickly.

That night Tony stared at the phone in his hand. He missed Isabelle more than he had ever thought possible.

To try to get her off his mind, he read through his texts, including one from his sister. Sydney was coming by to leave something wedding-related. The ceremony wasn't until June, yet Sydney was working on it whenever she had a chance. So far his folks were not participating or even attending. He was undecided whether to talk to them about it, or let it go by because it might be a more harmonious event for Sydney and Dylan if the senior Ryders weren't present.

Tony raked his hand through his hair, tangling it more. It was uncustomary for him to be so indecisive. He seemed to have lost his drive and he wasn't thinking clearly about big issues looming in his life.

Sydney breezed in, heading to his kitchen to spread brochures on the kitchen table. "This is where we're having the wedding. We've rented cottages nearby for the wedding party. I figured you would want your own place because I know how you like your privacy."

As she looked at him, her eyes narrowed. "Tony, are you all right?"

"Sure. Yes, I am. Just busy lately."

"You've been busy since you were eighteen years old." She walked around to feel his forehead and he pushed her hand away.

"Syd," he said in a threatening voice. "I'm okay. Stop that and let's get through this wedding stuff."

She placed her hands on her hips to look intently at him while her foot tapped. "Have you talked to Isabelle?"

"No. It's over between Isabelle and me. We're not talking at all."

"You really are in love with her," Sydney said, a note of wonder in her voice.

"I am not in love with Isabelle," Tony snapped, his temper rising. His sister was annoying him as she sometimes could and had since they were small kids. "Sydney, you're getting bratty."

"You're in love and you won't face up to it." When she giggled, he frowned, his cheeks burning and trying to hang on to his rising temper.

"My, oh, my. I knew this could happen, but I really expected you to make a bargain with some woman and have a marriage of convenience where you both profited from your union. I expected any marriage you would have would be a business contract. Instead, my brother is in love. Face it, Tony, you love her. What's so wrong about that? I know you're not holding out to marry one of those women our folks have picked out for you."

He glared at her. "Syd, you can be downright annoying sometimes. I thought you were outgrowing that, but you haven't. I'm not getting tied up in marriage until I reach my financial goals, and marriage is all Isabelle wants. End of story. We can't possibly be together."

Sydney laughed. "Of course you can be together. Why are you making yourself miserable, Tony? Wait until you see her someday with another man. You'll regret this beyond belief."

"I'm doing exactly what I want to do." He bit off his words, his anger increasing. "I have a goal of billionaire by forty. I have to keep Dad off my back and that will do it for all time. She has her own goal—marriage by thirty. Those goals are definitely not compatible. It's not like you and Dylan—you two *are* in love. We're not."

"I think you won't face the truth yourself." At his glare, she quickly added, "Hey, okay." And held up her hands as if surrendering. "Back to my wedding, then. Is this all right for a place for you to stay?" she asked, holding out a brochure.

"It's fine," he said, barely glancing at it. "You decide, Syd. All this wedding hoopla is not my deal. Do you need help paying for it? I'd be glad to."

She shook her head and gathered up the papers and brochures. "Thank you, Tony. Dylan wanted to pay for it. With you picking up my school tab, it's not placing him in a bind. Now remember, you wouldn't look at the brochures. I'll have to remind you that you told me to make the choices for you. Do you know how unlike you that is? Tony, face the truth. You're in love."

"So what if I am. I might be a little, but I want to reach my goal and that means staying single."

"You're not just a 'little' bit in love. I've never seen you like this. By the way, Isabelle very politely turned down my asking her to be a bridesmaid. She thought it would cause tension at my wedding. Actually, on the phone, she sounds as if she is getting along better than you are. Maybe she's met someone new."

"Sydney, dammit—"

She laughed. "Just pulling your chain. You are in king-size knots over Isabelle. You are in love and blind and in denial." She grabbed up her brochures to dash toward the door. "I'm going. Your choice though about love and marriage. I'll get out of your hair, which, by the way, is badly tangled."

"I didn't tell you how yours looked not long ago."

"That was sweet. Messy hair—mine, yours—both for the same reason."

"Syd—" he said threateningly, and she laughed, reaching for the door.

"See you later, Tony," she called over her shoulder, rushing out. He followed in long strides to watch her climb into her car and turn down his driveway. He waved, closed the door and walked back to his office with his mind on Isabelle and his sister's words ringing in his ears.

He was in love with her and he might as well face up to it. He was thinking about her most of his waking hours. He'd get over it and it wasn't that big a deal. As fast as that thought came, he could remember Isabelle's cutting remark about enjoying his money through the years and what an empty victory he would find it. Were his goals misplaced, blown all out of proportion? Was he ruining his life chasing the dollar when he was already enormously wealthy? The thought of seeing Isabelle with someone else chilled him. Sydney had put him in a sour mood, something she had rarely ever done.

It was even worse when he went to bed. He was lonely, missing Isabelle terribly. He picked up his phone and stared at her name at the head of his list of contacts. He wanted her, yet he always got over breakups, so the feeling of missing her should pass.

Right?

* * *

The following day at the office wasn't any better and then grew worse after the mail delivery. He looked at the thick cream-colored envelope in his hand. It had been opened in the mailroom and he slid out the announcement and invitation, scanning it swiftly, certain it was Isabelle's work.

It was from Tralear with Vernon's signature at the bottom inviting Tony to the Grand Opening Reception of the new Tralear Building under Vernon's new presidency. They would also introduce four new executives, including Isabelle.

Thinking about her, he hurt. How had she become so vital to him? Tony ran his hand over the embossed invitation, looking at the RSVP and then scrawling across it, "Please decline." He tossed it into a stack of mail for his secretary to handle. It was a week from Friday night. He thought about the sacrifices he had made, the long, grueling hours of work he had put in to become wealthy enough to keep his father off his back and to earn the man's respect. Was he sacrificing the love of his life for this goal? *Was* it going to be an empty victory? He missed her more each day. How much worse was it going to get? Was he losing the true love of his life?

He couldn't go back to letting his father constantly interfere with him, yet maybe he shouldn't worry about that and let it wreck his life. He missed and wanted Isabelle in his life. Tony made a mental note to get out of Dallas, go someplace away from work, where he could think straight about Isabelle and his future.

Isabelle couldn't resist stopping at the cubicle of the secretary who was keeping track of the reception RSVPs, and she learned that Tony had declined the invitation. Disappointment filled her even though it was what she had expected.

She missed him and the hurt wasn't lessening. There were moments now she was tempted to call him, accept his offer and forget her plans. She wouldn't meet someone else she wanted to marry. It was Tony she wanted and if not him...suddenly marriage didn't sound all that great.

Before long, the decision would be out of her hands, because he would find someone else. Tony would always have a woman in his life. On his terms.

The night of the reception, she dressed carefully, still wishing Tony would attend yet knowing he wouldn't be there. She had checked again yesterday to see if he possibly had changed his mind, but he had not and they were not letting anyone in who had not accepted the invitation.

She had bought a new red dress for the occasion. She wanted to wear black, but red would be more festive. She didn't feel festive. She simply hurt. She missed Tony and her friends at Ryder Enterprises, which she still thought of as Morris.

Her red dress had a plunging neckline and a low-cut back with tiny spaghetti straps and a straight short skirt. Thinking of Tony, she left her hair down and wore no jewelry.

The reception at the new Tralear Building was being held in a great room that would be used for such events or conferences. The tables were along the walls, covered in white cloths and holding a buffet of delicious food from steamy chicken and chilled shrimp to chocolate pastries and fruits. At one end of the room on a raised platform a band played. Guests mingled, filling the room with conversation and laughter.

She should have been jubilantly happy instead of wishing she were home and finding it difficult to carry on a conversation or even to listen to others.

Every tall man with black curly hair caught her attention. Because of the crowd, she could only see the top of one man's head, and his thick, black curls. She was mesmerized and couldn't look away because his hair reminded her of Tony. The resemblance made her heartbeat race. Would she be the same way about strangers who resembled him five years from now?

Should she rethink moving in with him? She knew it was too late to go back.

Then the man drew closer, the crowd parted and she looked into Tony's eyes.

Eleven

Her heart thudded and she forgot everything except Tony walking toward her, his gaze holding hers, immobilizing her. She smiled, but she was unable to speak. Her mouth went dry and she felt overwhelmed. She wanted to run and throw herself into his arms, but she maintained restraint. This was the time for that if she wanted him back. She felt that intuitively and thoroughly. It was also the time to get him out of her life forever if that was how it had to be.

He walked up to her. "Hi," he said, his thick, deep voice melting her. She couldn't even speak to answer him. "You're stunning," he said, his gaze roaming over her face and hair. "Where can we go to talk?"

"Tony, there's no point. I want all of you. I want marriage to you. I've made that clear and you've made your feelings clear to me. We should just stay in here. I need to greet people."

"I want to talk to you," he persisted.

"I'll be available tomorrow or the next day. I'm sure it can keep," she said, her pulse racing and her insides churning over rejecting him when he kept insisting on talking privately with her. She had spoken openly and frankly about her feelings. She saw no choice, except the one she had to live by.

She started to walk away from him. He pulled her around. When she began to protest, she took one look at his determined expression and closed her mouth.

"I have to talk to you."

"We really have nothing further to discuss."

"Yes, we do. I'm willing to give up my goal of billionaire by forty."

Stunned, she stood in shock, staring at him and trying to fathom what he had just stated. "You can't mean that," she said.

"I do mean it. Totally. I know what I want."

She stared at him, narrowing her eyes. "That is so totally unlike you in every way. I don't think you really can do it even if you think you mean it."

"I mean it, Isabelle, and I can do it if I really want it." He glanced around. "This isn't a good place to talk. The band is playing, people are beginning to dance around us."

She realized he was right. Her surroundings had faded into nonexistence for her. "All right, Tony, step into the hall. I didn't think you were coming tonight. I saw your RSVP."

"I didn't plan to attend and then at the last minute, I wanted to talk to you and I don't want to wait until tomorrow." He took her arm lightly, yet the touch made her draw a deep breath. She wanted to be in his arms more than ever. Her thoughts spun with his declaration of giving up his lifelong goal. She couldn't believe he actually would do so, but she was beginning to not care.

They walked into the hall and she looked up at him. "I have an office two stories down if you'd rather go there."

With his jaw set, he steered her toward the elevators and they rode in silence until they entered her office and he closed the door.

She walked away from him, turning to face him. "Tony, I

don't think you could live up to that even if you think you mean it now."

He closed the distance between them, stopping close to her. "My life is miserable without you in it. It isn't worth the sacrifice to stay single."

Surprised, she clamped her jaw shut tightly and shook her head. Tears threatened. She wanted to believe him, but she couldn't. "Tony, I've missed you, but you've spent your adult life as a workaholic, driven, addicted to work. I don't think you can change. You say you will, but several months after marriage or even a year or two later, your family will slip into second place. And you don't care for kids or really want children."

"Yes, I do. I want you and everything that goes with marriage to you. Kids—" He shrugged. "I don't know, but Sydney is younger than I am and I've always loved her."

"That's entirely different."

"Give me a chance here. I mean it. I want you in my life all the time. I want you enough to give up that goal of billionaire. If Dad threatens to cut me out of their will the way he has Sydney, that's fine. I'm a multimillionaire and I'll always work, but as far as being driven—I'm only driven to keep you in my life. I've put you first in my life." He reached for her, pulling her to him. "I've missed you a hell of a lot. I couldn't think of anything except missing you. When we were together I put you first in my life. You were still first in my life even when you were away from me. I don't want a life without you in it. No billionaire goal. Only family first, and by family, I mean you. I promise, Isabelle." He touched her hair lightly, brushing it away from her face. "I love you. Really love you. I've never been in love before. Nothing like this."

Her heart pounded with his declarations. Could she believe him? The words were magical, what she wanted to hear, but people rarely changed when personality and character and drive were involved.

"Tony, I desperately want to believe you, but people rarely change."

"Of course, they do, if they really want to. Addicts get over addiction. Smokers stop, alcoholics reform, people learn anger management, they get educations late in life when they realize they need them. People can change. Isabelle, I love you and I'll change for you. I'm putting you first right now." He reached into his pocket and pulled out a ring that sparkled in the light. Holding out the glittering ring, he knelt on one knee.

"I love you, Isabelle. Will you marry me and be my wife for all our lives? I promise to always put you and our family first because my love for you comes first."

Isabelle melted. "Yes, Tony," she whispered, her heart thudding as she took the ring with its huge diamond, surrounded by other diamonds. "Tony," she whispered, looking up at him as he stood to embrace her. "I love you. I have for so long."

Tears spilled over and he wiped them away. "Don't cry," he said, gazing into her eyes and then at her mouth. As she stood on tiptoe to kiss him, he leaned down and kissed her.

Her heart pounded with joy as he slid the ring on her finger. She knew she was taking a chance, but was willing to do so because Tony was willing to take a chance also.

"Let's have this wedding soon," he whispered, pausing to look into her eyes. "I don't want to wait until June the way Sydney is."

"I agree," she whispered. "Are you going to let me keep my goal?"

"Definitely. I'm going to help you achieve it."

She smiled at him and then they kissed.

Twelve

At the wedding reception at their country club in Dallas, Isabelle danced with her new husband. She had shed the long satin train to her dress, which was plain lines with a strapless top and a straight skirt. Tony took her breath away in his dark tuxedo, and the look of love in his eyes kept her warm.

It was May with flowers in bloom. The world looked beautiful to her and her love made her smile constantly.

"Your family is nice, Isabelle. Mine could take a lesson."

"Your parents have been nice to me, Tony," she said, glancing briefly at the guests surrounding the dance floor.

"They've given up. Maybe it's old age, maybe hope of a grandchild. They're even going to Syd's wedding and Dad will give her away. They just told her last night at our rehearsal dinner."

Isabel beamed. "I'm so glad."

He smiled. "You are really into families. I've never asked how many kids you want and I suspect I may have to brace myself for the answer," he said teasingly, holding her lightly as they danced around the floor.

"I really never had a set number in mind. I grew up in a big family. It was fun. Let's think about three for a start."

"Start and maybe finish. I can't see myself coaching soccer, but I'm willing to give it a try."

"I can definitely see you doing that, taking charge, making it all run smoothly and helping little kids."

He laughed. "Right now, I want to dance you right out of the door and to the limo and away to where I'll have you to myself for the next three weeks."

She smiled at her handsome husband. "That you can do later. Right now we finish the dance and then I dance with my dad and your father and Dylan and maybe some of your friends and Vernon and Mr. Morris—"

"Stop. I know the drill. Weddings, protocol, ritual, routines—I just want to dream about five hours from now."

A half hour later, Tony stood with his friends.

"Gabe, here's a toast to you. You're the last bachelor, which we knew you would be. You've escaped your dad's meddling and now all our fathers have reformed," Tony said.

"In short," Nick added, "you've led a charmed life. Jake has paved the way for you, helped in some of your fights growing up. What a cushy life you have."

"Beside that," Tony chimed in, "you love that ranch you have and you don't get any flack from your dad. Imagine if any of us had tried to become a cowboy—the blowup and threats would have been monumental."

Gabe grinned and raised the flute of champagne that had barely been touched. "Thanks, guys. I don't know that my life is quite that charmed, but I've been lucky. I still enjoy being single. I definitely enjoy my ranch life, plus the fact that Dad leaves me alone. I do feel a little lucky."

"To the golden boy," Jake said, "my kid brother." They all sipped.

"There is cold beer at the bar if any of you want to get rid of this," Tony said, and Gabe nodded. "If you guys will excuse me, I've been away from my bride a long time now."

"All of half an hour," Jake remarked dryly, and they laughed as Tony left them.

His heart filled with joy at the sight of Isabelle. She had never looked more beautiful than today and he wanted to whisk her away from here and leave for their honeymoon. Before heading to Paris, they were spending four days in New York City and he had no intention of leaving their hotel suite. He was overjoyed to have her to himself, wondering why he had ever thought making a bigger fortune was more important than having her in his life. He watched as Sydney stood talking to her. He was happy for his sister, too, who was so much in love she couldn't stop smiling. He could understand her feelings now.

He walked up to slip his arm around Isabelle's tiny waist.

"Can I steal my bride away?" he asked the group, and without hearing their answers, he led Isabelle away. "Can we leave?"

"Not a moment too soon," she whispered, smiling at him. "My clothes are on your plane and I can just go. I said my goodbyes to everyone earlier."

"So did I," Tony replied, his heartbeat speeding as they headed for a door.

Hours later Tony carried Isabelle over the threshold of their hotel room. He set her on her feet, kicking the door closed while he kissed her.

Holding him tightly, she wound her fingers in his thick black curls. Her heart pounded with joy. She pushed away his tuxedo coat and it fell unnoticed on the floor.

"Tony, there are moments I can't believe all this is really happening," she whispered as she felt his fingers at the buttons of her pale blue dress.

"It's real, love. I'll show you and I'll spend my life trying to make you happy and be the husband, lover, father you want. You're first in my life, Isabelle," he stated solemnly. "Always first. It couldn't possibly be any other way. I can't tell you the joy you give me, but I'm going to try to show you, every way I can."

She smiled at him. "You already have in so many ways," she whispered, fingering the diamond-and-sapphire necklace he had given her as a wedding gift. Her conversation ended as they kissed and she held him tightly. Happiness consumed her. His dark eyes proclaimed his love with unmistakable warmth.

"Tony, I love you with all my heart. My joy is complete in you," she whispered, and returned to kissing him again.

The future looked filled with promises of hope, fulfillment and dreams come true.

* * * * *

Harlequin®

Desire

COMING NEXT MONTH
Available August 9, 2011

You can find more information on upcoming
Harlequin® titles, free excerpts and more at
www.HarlequinInsideRomance.com.

REQUEST YOUR FREE BOOKS!

2 FREE NOVELS PLUS 2 FREE GIFTS!

⬧ Harlequin®

Desire

ALWAYS POWERFUL, PASSIONATE AND PROVOCATIVE

YES! Please send me 2 FREE Harlequin Desire® novels and my 2 FREE gifts (gifts are worth about $10). After receiving them, if I don't wish to receive any more books, I can return the shipping statement marked "cancel." If I don't cancel, I will receive 6 brand-new novels every month and be billed just $4.30 per book in the U.S. or $4.99 per book in Canada. That's a saving of at least 14% off the cover price! It's quite a bargain! Shipping and handling is just 50¢ per book in the U.S. and 75¢ per book in Canada.* I understand that accepting the 2 free books and gifts places me under no obligation to buy anything. I can always return a shipment and cancel at any time. Even if I never buy another book, the two free books and gifts are mine to keep forever.

225/326 HDN FEF3

Name _____ (PLEASE PRINT) _____

Address _____ Apt. # _____

City _____ State/Prov. _____ Zip/Postal Code _____

Signature (if under 18, a parent or guardian must sign)

Mail to the **Reader Service:**

IN U.S.A.: P.O. Box 1867, Buffalo, NY 14240-1867
IN CANADA: P.O. Box 609, Fort Erie, Ontario L2A 5X3

Not valid for current subscribers to Harlequin Desire books.

**Want to try two free books from another line?
Call 1-800-873-8635 or visit www.ReaderService.com.**

---

* Terms and prices subject to change without notice. Prices do not include applicable taxes. Sales tax applicable in N.Y. Canadian residents will be charged applicable taxes. Offer not valid in Quebec. This offer is limited to one order per household. All orders subject to credit approval. Credit or debit balances in a customer's account(s) may be offset by any other outstanding balance owed by or to the customer. Please allow 4 to 6 weeks for delivery. Offer available while quantities last.

Your Privacy—The Reader Service is committed to protecting your privacy. Our Privacy Policy is available online at www.ReaderService.com or upon request from the Reader Service.

We make a portion of our mailing list available to reputable third parties that offer products we believe may interest you. If you prefer that we not exchange your name with third parties, or if you wish to clarify or modify your communication preferences, please visit us at www.ReaderService.com/consumerschoice or write to us at Reader Service Preference Service, P.O. Box 9062, Buffalo, NY 14269. Include your complete name and address.

HDES11B

*Once bitten, twice shy. That's Gabby Wade's motto—
especially when it comes to Adamson men.
And the moment she meets Jon Adamson her theory
is confirmed. But with each encounter a little* something
*sparks between them, making her wonder if she's been
too hasty to dismiss this one!*

*Enjoy this sneak peek from ONE GOOD REASON
by Sarah Mayberry, available August 2011
from Harlequin® Superromance®.*

Gabby Wade's heartbeat thumped in her ears as she marched to her office. She wanted to pretend it was because of her brisk pace returning from the file room, but she wasn't that good a liar.

Her heart was beating like a tom-tom because Jon Adamson had touched her. In a very male, very possessive way. She could still feel the heat of his big hand burning through the seat of her khakis as he'd steadied her on the ladder.

It had taken every ounce of self-control to tell him to unhand her. What she'd really wanted was to grab him by his shirt and, well, explore all those urges his touch had instantly brought to life.

While she might not like him, she was wise enough to understand that it wasn't always about liking the other person. Sometimes it was about pure animal attraction.

Refusing to think about it, she turned to work. When she'd typed in the wrong figures three times, Gabby admitted she was too tired and too distracted. Time to call it a day.

As she was leaving, she spied Jon at his workbench in the shop. His head was propped on his hand as he studied blueprints. It wasn't until she got closer that she saw his eyes were shut.

He looked oddly boyish. There was something innocent and unguarded in his expression. She felt a weakening in her resistance to him.

"Jon." She put her hand on his shoulder, intending to shake him awake. Instead, it rested there like a caress.

His eyes snapped open.

"You were asleep."

"No, I was, uh, visualizing something on this design." He gestured to the blueprint in front of him then rubbed his eyes.

That gesture dealt a bigger blow to her resistance. She realized it wasn't only animal attraction pulling them together. She took a step backward as if to get away from the knowledge.

She cleared her throat. "I'm heading off now."

He gave her a smile, and she could see his exhaustion.

"Yeah, I should, too." He stood and stretched. The hem of his T-shirt rose as he arched his back and she caught a flash of hard male belly. She looked away, but it was too late. Her mind had committed the image to permanent memory.

And suddenly she knew, for good or bad, she'd never look at Jon the same way again.

Find out what happens next in ONE GOOD REASON, available August 2011 from Harlequin® Superromance®!

Celebrating

Blaze **10** *years of*
red-hot reads

Featuring a special August author lineup of
six fan-favorite authors who have written
for Blaze™ from the beginning!

The Original Sexy Six:

Vicki Lewis Thompson
Tori Carrington
Kimberly Raye
Debbi Rawlins
Julie Leto
Jo Leigh

Pick up all six Blaze™
Special Collectors' Edition titles!

August 2011

Plus visit
HarlequinInsideRomance.com
and click on the Series Excitement Tab
for exclusive Blaze™ 10th Anniversary content!

www.Harlequin.com